Betti
on the
High Wire

DIAL BOOKS FOR YOUNG READERS
A division of Penguin Young Readers Group
Published by The Penguin Group
Penguin Group (USA) Inc., 375 Hudson Street, New York, NY 10014, U.S.A.
Penguin Group (Canada), 90 Eglinton Avenue East, Suite 700, Toronto, Ontario,
Canada M4P 2Y3 (a division of Pearson Penguin Canada Inc.)
Penguin Books Ltd, 80 Strand, London WC2R 0RL, England
Penguin Ireland, 25 St. Stephen's Green, Dublin 2, Ireland (a division of Penguin
Books Ltd)
Penguin Group (Australia), 250 Camberwell Road, Camberwell, Victoria 3124,
Australia (a division of Pearson Australia Group Pty Ltd)
Penguin Books India Pvt Ltd, 11 Community Centre, Panchsheel Park, New
Delhi - 110 017, India
Penguin Group (NZ), 67 Apollo Drive, Rosedale, North Shore 0632, New
Zealand (a division of Pearson New Zealand Ltd)
Penguin Books (South Africa) (Pty) Ltd, 24 Sturdee Avenue, Rosebank,
Johannesburg 2196, South Africa
Penguin Books Ltd, Registered Offices: 80 Strand, London WC2R 0RL, England

Designed by Jennifer Kelly
Text set in New Caledonia

Printed in the U.S.A.

10 9 8 7 6 5 4 3 2 1

Library of Congress Cataloging-in-Publication Data
Railsback, Lisa.
Betti on the high wire / by Lisa Railsback.
cm.
Summary: Firm in her belief that her missing parents will return to the bombed-
out circus camp where she lives with a group of "leftover" children, ten-year-old
Babo has no desire to leave her war-torn country.
   ISBN 978-0-8037-3388-6 (hardcover)
[1. Abandoned children—Fiction. 2. People with disabilities—Fiction.
3. War—Fiction. 4. Conduct of life—Fiction.] I. Title.
   PZ7.R1287 Be 2010
   [Fic]—dc22   2009040046

Betti on the High Wire

by Lisa Railsback

DIAL BOOKS FOR YOUNG READERS
an imprint of Penguin Group (USA) Inc.

FOR
THE GREAT FISH

My Circus Life

A bright light shines on the beautiful girl. Everyone is watching as she walks carefully on a line that goes up into the sky. Her mama smiles at the top. Her mama is the Tallest Woman in the World with a Tail. And her dad, the famous Green Alligator Man, waits below. They will catch the beautiful girl if she ever falls. But she never falls, of course. She's a circus star.

The audience claps and claps every night and shouts for more. They shout for her to keep going, to go higher, to touch a fancy bird in another sky. The beautiful girl is brave. And they love her because she makes them forget things . . . for just a minute or two.

❁　　❁　　❁

MOST OF THE leftover kids have nightmares. But me? I dream about the circus.

My name is Babo.

The leftover kids call me Big Mouth Babo because I have an opinion—or a Big Mouth story—for just about everything. They like my circus stories best. By now they feel like they practically know the Hairy Bear Boy and the clowns who all have red hair and the Snake Lady and the Teeny-Tiny Puppet Man and the rest.

They especially love the long story about my mama, the Tallest Woman in the World with a Tail, and my dad, the bumpy Green Alligator Man. This story, I tell them, is absolutely true, and it will definitely have a happy ending once the war cools off and the circus comes back again.

And the true story about me? Well, my story started when Auntie Moo spotted me alone at the empty circus camp when I was about three. Now I'm about ten, I think. Auntie Moo found me eating lizards and drinking rainwater from the elephant bowl, toddling around just like I owned the place. Pots and pans littered the ground, old makeup was thrown in the dirt, and the canvas circus tents were flaming like a bonfire.

Auntie Moo named me Babo and the name stuck, and I've been at the empty circus camp ever since. She got stuck too, sort of. You can't exactly leave a toddler toddling around by herself, especially during a war. And before long, more leftover kids were left here, so we were all stuck together.

I've asked Auntie Moo at least a hundred times about what happened to the circus. She says that the soldiers were probably afraid of the circus freaks, so they burned everything down. But while things were burning, three of the soldiers got squished by the elephant, one soldier got chewed by the lion, one got squeezed to death by the big snake, and another got swallowed. And the circus animals and the circus people disappeared.

That's why the villagers say our circus camp is haunted.

They say that circus ghosts are still flying all over the place. They can still hear the circus music floating through the woods on windy nights. Sometimes they think they hear gasps and claps from the audience, and faint, happy singing from the circus people. The villagers won't visit our circus camp because they're afraid.

That's what happens during a war. Everyone is afraid of everything.

But I've been here forever and I'm not afraid, even though sometimes I hear the old circus music too. I'll never be afraid because I was here first, so that makes me the leader. I'm the brave one. Besides, there's nothing left for soldiers to take and nothing left for them to burn. And nobody cares about the leftover kids at the leftover circus camp anyway.

Nobody except my mama and dad, of course. All I know is that they must've left me here because they had to. Because they'd be back to get me any day.

Bad Eyes and Short Toes

"PSSST. GEORGE?"

I was the only one awake when the sun hadn't started beating down on us yet. We slept in the old lion's cage because that's where we could all fit. It was the best animal cage out of all of them because we could see straight up to the sky, so we always knew if something was coming.

"George! Can you hear it?"

"Go back to sleep, Babo."

George was taking up too much space, like a little pig. His arm flung out to the side and his legs were split like a wishbone. The rest of us were crunched into the corner, as usual. Nine of us, but there used to be ten before the foreigners started coming.

"It's another one."

"I don't hear anything, Babo."

"George, wake up! I'm sure. There's another one coming."

George rolled over and covered his face with his potato sack. He mumbled something, but I couldn't understand. George didn't like mornings, and on this morning, sure enough, it was going to be impossible to sleep. Because I was right.

The bars of the lion cage started shaking and the sky was grumbling like a noisy monsoon.

I covered my ears and pointed up. "See? George, look!"

George finally sat up and rubbed his eyes with his hand. "Oh!" He jumped to his feet and hiked up his baggy shorts. "You're right, Babo!" He waved his potato sack in the air like a flag. "It *is* a plane!"

The little ones started waving too. Some of them were so excited that they had to jump up and down while the wind was blowing their hair all over the place. "Hallooooo, Foreeeenerz. Hallooooo!" they shouted in so-called English. I rolled my eyes. I was the only smart one who knew that you say "hello" and not "hallooo" and that not a single foreigner could hear from so high up in an airplane.

"Stop waving!" I hollered. "We don't *want* them to come here! REMEMBER?"

The noise was so loud that none of the leftover kids could hear me. Or they didn't want to hear me. So I shouted again: "STOP! STOP IT! STOP!"

And finally, that lousy plane was gone. It left a dusty cloudy trail in the sky and George kept staring up and smiling, even though the sun was hitting him straight in the eyes.

"STOP!" I cried louder, but they had already stopped and everything was already quiet.

George looked at me with his dark eyes and tilted his head. "Why, Babo?" His potato sack dropped to the floor. "Why don't you want the foreigners to help us?"

"You really think the Melons want to *help* us, George?" *The Melons* was my very special name for the foreigners. They usually had pink faces, and everyone from my country, especially at the market, tried to squeeze money out of them like juice. I took a deep breath and started pacing back and forth. Being the leader was such a big responsibility. "I already told you. A million times. You think they're *nice*?"

George nodded, a little.

I laughed dramatically. "George . . ."

George's eyes got huge and he backed up.

"Do you understand what happens to leftover kids once they're in a foreign country? Do you?"

He shook his head.

"Well, for one, those countries are always way too big. If you get lost, you'll never find your way home. *Lost forever*. And the Melons? They're so used to getting new things and throwing out old things that they wouldn't even *care* if you got lost. That's what Old Lady

Suri at the bean stand said. They'd just get a brand-new kid. Just like that."

George gulped.

"And . . . if you say something wrong? If you say 'horse' when you mean to say 'mama'? Do you know what those foreigners do?" I swung around and looked all the kids straight in the eye. They bit at their dirty fingernails and shuffled their feet. "They throw you behind bars!" I pointed at the bars to make my point.

"Like the lion cage?" asked George in a tiny voice.

"Worse. Much much worse. They call it 'zoo,' and normal Melon kids come and stare at you. And laugh. And you're locked in forever." I put my hand over my good eye and bugged out my bad one. I made funny sounds and shook at the bars of the lion cage. "And another thing," I said, "is if you have a Big Mouth. If you talk too much and tell too many stories and you tell the Melon children all the secrets about the war—or the circus—well, they put your whole face in a square box."

"In a box?" squeaked George.

"They call it a 'telee-vi-zion.' It's scary, George."

"They laugh at my face?"

"I'm afraid so."

"You made that up, right?" George tried to follow me back and forth, but he kept running into my heels. "Did you hear that from Old Lady Suri too? That's just a story, Babo. Right?"

I shrugged mysteriously.

George was worried. He crinkled his eyes. "It is, isn't it?"

"Maybe. Maybe not. But worst of all, George?" I stopped pacing and thought about things. "Is when they try to turn you into a Melon. Just like them. They take your head and turn it inside out so you can't even remember who you are."

"Inside out? My head?" George itched his head.

"You'll walk differently and you'll dress differently and you'll eat scary food. Even your face will look different, George. The Melons make you take baths, and they scrub and scrub and scrub you clean until you're blue and raw and wrinkled like a baby elephant. See, they make you forget everything. They make you forget where your *real* home is. Even your *real* parents!"

Most of the leftover kids couldn't remember their real parents anyway, but that didn't matter a bit.

Just then Auntie Moo rushed over and called, "Hurry, children! We have to hurry! The foreigners are coming today!"

And that was the end of my important lessons.

Auntie Moo had been sound asleep by the fire circle when the plane flew over us. She wiped her perfectly clean hands against her faded skirt and said, "I didn't know they were coming so soon." She shook her head, and her long gray braid shook too.

"The Melons?" I groaned. "Not here. Not again."

"Babo . . ." Auntie Moo gave me a sly smile. She didn't like my special nickname a bit.

"I know."

"You need to put on your special occasion clothes. We'll wash the dirt off and comb your hair."

The leftover kids forgot my lessons in about one second, because they ran out of the lion cage as if they were about to meet some royal princess. All of them except for George. He was still sitting in the corner. He was upset about zoos and boxes and getting lost.

And me? I moaned, "But whyyy?"

"Why, why," Auntie Moo laughed. "Because, Babo. We want you to have a chance to go to another country. That's all."

"*Why* would I want to do *that*?"

Auntie Moo laid one hand on my shoulder and pointed at the ground with her other hand. I sat down and she sat next to me. "You'll go to school there," Auntie Moo explained in her very soft voice. George listened too. "You'll have a family, Babo, and a home. All sorts of food, and—"

"A 'better life,' I know." I folded my arms across my chest and kicked my bare heels. "Well, I have a good enough life already. And you're my school. So I don't WANT to go!"

"Babo," Auntie Moo sighed as usual and brushed hair out of my eyes. "We don't have much time."

Lucky Snake

THE LEFTOVER KIDS were running around like crazy.
They were combing their hair and washing their faces
and scrubbing the dirt off their toes. This was their big
chance. They wanted to be adopted.

"Big deal," I mumbled as I walked to the river with
my special occasion dress thrown over my shoulder. My
enormous dress was the most special of all. Auntie Moo
had found it crunched up in a ball after the soldiers
burned the circus camp down. It was sun-faded orange,
even though it used to be red. There were holes in the
sleeves and around the neck, and the bottom of it was
jaggedy with thread strings hanging off like moss. A few
tiny silver sparkles barely clung on and glittered when I
pretended to be a star in front of the fire circle.

I held my special occasion dress very, very carefully

as I hopped over patches of prickly vines. The Melons could never understand how special it was.

THE WAR HAS been my country's bad luck for so long that no one remembers exactly how it started. Things keep getting blown up and rebuilt, and blown up and rebuilt, so we've all just gotten used to holey roofs and skeleton walls. Then the war got worse and the foreigners wanted to help. They even want to help us, the leftover children. Or that's what they say.

"Wait, Babo. Wait for me!"

George was running after me as usual. He was just about the slowest runner in the whole world.

"Can I wash my clothes with you?"

"Sure." I shrugged as I reached the bank of the river and kneeled down. "But it's a big fat waste of our time, George." I plugged my nose and dipped the sleeve of my dress in the water. "The Melons won't adopt us anyway. You know how it is. They always want the pretty children."

George plunked himself down next to me. His bottom lip stuck out like he was about to cry. With his special occasion shirt in his hand, George tried to see his face in the murky water. The water was even dirtier than usual because our village hadn't had any rain for a month; the pigs and the people still had to wash in it, rain or no rain.

"That's just the way it is," I told him. "They want the children who have all their fingers and toes."

"What about Sela, Babo? She got adopted. She was one of us."

"Sela was a *pretty* one. The foreigners loved her pretty curls, remember? And her eyes? She didn't have a single thing wrong with her, George. Prettier than all of us put together. Remember?"

George nodded and we were quiet. He dunked his whole shirt in the water and swished it back and forth.

We know we aren't the pretty ones.

Both of my eyes are the color of smoke or a gray rainy day. But one of them doesn't work. It stares off like a washed-up fish. I'm also missing my big toe on one foot and my baby toes on both. No one notices my missing toes very often because my toes are dirty and people probably just think I have little feet. Besides, most people in our country are missing at least one finger or toe, so I'm not strange.

Auntie Moo said I'd be fine without all my toes. The only reason I'd need them, she said, was if I lost both of my hands and would need to write urgent messages with my toes. I hope this will never happen.

My hair is a funny color—a mishmash of colors, really—and it goes crazy every morning and flies all over the place. Sister Baroo from the Mission grumbles and swears when she tries to comb my hair for the foreigners. She says that my hair is way too wild, but Auntie Moo says that it's very unique. I say that only circus people have hair like mine.

I'm skinny too. My ribs stick out like a skin-'n'-bones chicken. It's not pretty when a girl looks hungry all the time. But I don't complain because some of the other leftover kids have it worse. George is missing an arm and has extra-large ears, Toro's hearing is messed up, and a couple of kids got knocked in the head so their brains are out of order. Almost everybody has one broken thing or another, but that's what happens during a war.

Once I asked Auntie Moo what happened to my eye and she said it was hard to know for sure. Maybe I was born this way. Or maybe it happened in the war, or maybe it happened in the circus a long, long time ago.

"Maybe the foreigners won't care if your eye is broken, Babo," said George. He sighed and looked down at himself. "Maybe they won't care about my arm."

"Maybe," I said. "It doesn't really matter anyway."

George was having a hard time getting the dirt out of his good shirt, so I took it out of his hand and beat it on the side of a rock. Water flew all over us and we shook it off like wet dogs. George giggled.

"There." I grinned. "Good enough."

LATER WE WERE all getting fidgety in our special occasion clothes. There was only so long we could wait politely for the Melons. And that's when Auntie Moo asked me if I would play a quiet game with the leftover children.

"But, Babo"—Auntie Moo smiled slyly—"try not to get them dirty? Like last time?"

Last time I made them perform like my dad, the famous alligator man, with flips and flops in the murky swamp halfway down to the village. Hundreds of frogs and bugs bounced on top of the furry algae. That time the leftover kids' hair was all green for the Melons, which I thought was very, very funny.

The time before that, I made up a game where black-bottomed circus monkeys took over the world. I told the leftover kids to put a little mud on their faces—just a lit-tle—to look like monkeys. Then we hid in the trees and dropped onto my pretend soldiers, Toro and George. We dragged the soldiers into the Hairy Bear Boy's old skel-eton of a tent, where I made them do headstands and we tickled their toes. But that time Toro got a black eye and the leftover kids had a mud fight and soon mud was dried all over our monkey faces like chipped cement. I thought we didn't look so bad when the Melons arrived, but Sister Baroo didn't think it was a bit funny. She made me sit on the Mission floor in the village and pray for three hours that I wouldn't be so bad next time.

Sister Baroo always wants to help us too, just like the Melons. She runs the Mission down in the village, which used to feed all the poor people. Before the poor people could eat their free meal, Sister Baroo would make them take baths in a big rusty water trough and comb their hair and pray for three hours on the Mission floor. They had to pray that they'd be able to pay for their own food and have cleaner lives in the near future. So the poor people got fed up with Sister Baroo and decided that they'd rather live dirty and hungry in the street. That's when the circus camp and the leftover children became Sister Baroo's new mission. Just our luck.

Sister Baroo wouldn't like my new game at all. This time I tied an old rag over George's eyes. "Now, you're the animal trainer, George," I told him. "And the rest of us are the circus animals. But we're mad at you. So we refuse to do any more shows."

"Why, Babo?" George tilted his head.

"Because," I said, "you make us get clean, and you comb our hair, and you make us perform for the fancy Melons. Every night. So we want a vacation."

George pulled the rag off his eyes. "I would never be mean to the circus animals, Babo."

"George! It's just a game!" I pulled the rag back down. "Do you want to play, or not?"

"Yes, but I don't want to be the animal trainer. He's mean." George frowned. He didn't like mean people. "What do the animals do to me, Babo?"

"We run away. And you have to find us."

"But—"

"Okay, GO!" I shouted.

All of us started crawling around. Crawling around a little couldn't get us too dirty. We were funny monkeys and rainbow birds and singing lions and hairy bear boys and dancing elephants.

"Miss Lion?" called George, still standing in the same exact spot. He stretched his arm out. "Bird? Here, Mister Bird!" He twirled in funny circles, while the rest of us covered our mouths so we wouldn't laugh.

Then I had a brilliant idea. I made the leftover kids crawl behind me into the pig yard. The pigs were drinking at the river, so they couldn't get us dirty. "Sssss. Sssss." We teased George like snakes. "ROARRRRR." We sang like lions, we spoke in funny languages like exotic birds, and George tried to follow us. "Caw caw, cheep cheep, grrrrrrrr."

"Here, animals!" cried George. "Don't run away!"

We all hid behind the pig trough that Auntie Moo filled with slop. "Don't touch it!" I whispered to the kids who were dipping their fingers already. "We can't get dirty! Not now."

George heard my whispering and he smiled.

I'd never seen him move so fast. He marched straight for the trough with his arm out. His bare feet stepped right into a pig pile, but he didn't care. "Babo?" he called. "Caw caw?"

The rest of us ducked down, and there was . . . silence.

"George?" I stood up and looked around. He wasn't anywhere. "George!"

Just then, from the woods, we heard Sister Baroo. "CHILDREN!" she hollered in her husky, irritated voice. "Babo!"

George suddenly stood up from the other side of the pig trough and scared me so much that I screamed.

"Look, Babo! I trained a circus animal!" George proudly puffed out his chest and handed me his animal. Six feet long and thicker than a leftover kid. I screamed like crazy and threw the huge snake into the air. It conked its head on a branch, spun around, and landed in a spooky lump on a pig pile. Then I accidentally crashed into the pig trough, which tipped straight over and covered us all in sloppy slop.

George plopped down to check on his snake because he was worried about it. And me? I RAN. The other kids chased after me through the woods, leaping over brambles and baby monkeys. I was running so fast that I forgot all about Sister Baroo, who'd stomped up from the village in her black boots and her boring black dress.

Unfortunately, I tripped at exactly the wrong second and crashed straight into Sister Baroo and her basket of eggs. The eggs flew out of her hand, into the air, and *splat*. All over her. A piece of eggshell sat on the tip of her nose.

"Babo, you are clumsier than a pig in mud," hissed Sister Baroo. "Those eggs were for the foreigners' dinner!"

I shrugged. Then I stared at her eggshell nose. I tried not to giggle because that's when she gets really mad. She started making wild jerks with her head, and then I saw them. The Melons were standing right behind her! Six of them.

Kids probably never got so dirty in their country. Perfect.

The younger children pulled on the bottom of Baroo's messy dress and told her about George's snake. Her eyes lit up. She stomped with her big feet to the pig trough, where George was petting the snake as if it was his best friend.

"This is a special snake, children," said Sister Baroo.

We all bent over and looked closer. It didn't look that special to me; a snake is a snake.

"My mother said there's only one that slithers into your life," she continued. "Just one time. And it means good luck."

"Really?" I asked. "Who gets the good luck?"

"It's hard to say," answered Sister Baroo, finally flicking that eggshell off her nose. "Actually, it could mean bad luck too. It's hard to say."

Monkeys and Melons

THE MELONS DIDN'T like the snake whether it was lucky or not. They politely pushed it around on their banana leaf plates as they talked to Auntie Moo and Sister Baroo. They pretended to chew as they nodded and smiled.

The Melons were dressed in clean clothes and they all wore shoes. The women were fanning themselves with banana leaves and the men's faces were red and drippy. None of them were used to our heat.

One of the ladies had hair that rose up on top of her head like a bright yellow tree. She had clips in it so it wouldn't fall down in a storm, and I kept thinking about all the things that could get stuck in hair like that. Birds could build nests, and weeds could grow from the roots, and monkeys could pick nits from yellow knots.

One man had a large nose, with a little orange mustache between his nose and his mouth. He had a few strands of flying hair on his head, but mostly he was bald. Another woman had lips painted red, the same color to match her fingernails and her dress.

But I was most curious about a quiet couple that sat at the very end of the log actually chewing on their snake.

I couldn't see so well, but I thought that the snake-eating lady smiled at me. I hid my face behind George.

"What's the matter, Babo?" George whispered. "These foreigners seem very nice."

I didn't answer because my mouth was full.

The Melons didn't even know how to speak our language. The quiet couple tried a few words—how are you, are you hungry, what is your name—but the left-over kids had no idea what the Melon couple was trying to say and the Melon couple had no idea what the left-over kids were trying to say. Auntie Moo was trying her best to translate everyone's messy language, but really I thought they all should've stayed quiet and eaten their snake.

I spoke English pretty well and understood a lot of it, just like Auntie Moo.

She gave all of us English lessons three times a week, because she thought it might be important someday. But the kids with out-of-order brains couldn't pay attention, and Toro couldn't hear, and most of the others couldn't understand that our language wasn't the only language in the whole world.

I practiced English with Auntie Moo almost every night after the leftover kids fell asleep. We practiced speaking to each other, and we practiced reading and writing from an old English book that was donated to the Mission, and we practiced new important words like "nation" and "war" and "bananas" and "soldier" and "ghosts" and "eye" and "independence" and "broken" and "pig." Auntie Moo said that I passed her up in English a long time ago.

George studied very hard, but he still wasn't nearly as smart as me. He always tried to speak English to the Melons. But me? I didn't have much to say.

After dinner the Melons got a tour of the circus camp. It started with me in the ticket booth—basically a tiny falling-down shack—at the entrance. I stood in the window and asked for donations for the tour. The Melons always opened their moneybags and gave me money, even though Auntie Moo hated it when I asked for money from the Melons. But I told her that the leftover kids deserved to get something because we always got clean for the Melons and we never got anything back. I whispered to each Melon to be careful because our circus camp was haunted. Then I gave each of them a banana, which Toro took back again as their tickets.

I loved the Melon tours.

Old Lady Suri from the bean stand told me everything I needed to know about how the circus used to
be. And I, of course, told the important stories to the
leftover kids.

Exotic birds greeted the audience as they walked
through the ticket booth and down the path to the
elephant ring. The birds knew words in three different languages and there was even a Bird Woman with a
beak, who flapped her wings and laid large exotic eggs
in front of the audience.

The elephant ring was in the center of the camp.
The famous elephant named Fifi wore an extra-large
fancy suit and did tricks in the ring, like somersaults
and backflips. Circus clowns with red hair rode on Fifi
and sometimes there was a tower of clowns standing
tall as a house on the elephant's back. As a special treat
Fifi would pick up a log where five audience members
were sitting and raise it high into the sky.

There were all sorts of other things happening at the
circus too, so the audience never got bored. On one
side of the circus camp they could view all the circus
animals.

Monkey People in tall hats twirled sticks of fire and
then chomped on the sticks until their black faces
and their black bottoms turned red. They swung
back and forth from the trees by their feet, sold
snacks, and asked for tips in their hats.

The audience could walk straight into the pigpen, where there was a special pig with five heads. The audience got to pay money to feed sloppy slop to all of her two-headed piglets. The lion named Cindi was a favorite too. Mostly Cindi roamed around the audience and nuzzled them like a kitten, but at night she'd go into her lion cage. Instead of roaring, she'd sing love songs to her lion mate who was lost in the jungle.

The Snake Lady lived with all of her snakes in a tree house behind the circus animals. Her hair hung down to the bottom of the tree, so all the snakes lived in her hair and in the tree, and you couldn't tell the difference. If the audience was lucky, and if the Snake Lady was in a good mood, they'd see her do a special dance. Her snakes all moved back and forth to the same rhythm, rattling out the beat. The Snake Lady didn't speak any words. She just spoke snake: *Sssssss. Sssssss.*

The circus people lived on the far side of the circus camp, along the path that went to the river. There used to be lots of tents, red and yellow and green. Now there were just ratty pole branches that leaned, with pieces of dirty cloth blowing from the tops. The fire circle was in front of the tents. That's where all the fun happened, said Old Lady Suri, after the audience had gone away late at night.

The Teeny-Tiny Puppet Man acted out all sorts of roles for his comical puppet shows in one of the old tents. His little head would bop up and down on the puppet stage as he changed characters and voices. Somehow, said Old Lady Suri, he made stories about the war very, very funny.

The Hairy Bear Boy told fortunes in another tent to anyone who would listen. The trouble was that not many audience members wanted to listen because the Hairy Bear Boy didn't exactly like being so hairy. He was a bit sour and beat his chest a lot. All of his fortunes had to do with people getting smooshed or eaten or stomped on in life.

Of course the Melons visiting the circus camp nowadays didn't get to see or know anything about the real circus. The leftover kids gave the tours and they couldn't even speak English. They just pointed at things. They also tried to act like Cindi the lion in the lion cage, and the Hairy Bear Boy, and the Teeny-Tiny Puppet Man, and the Snake Lady, even though the Melons had no idea what they were watching.

I'd only taught the leftover kids the important English words. Toro liked to point out where the soldiers got smooshed and swallowed in front of the fire circle. He stated proudly: "Soldier eaten here," and "Soldier stomped by FiFi," and "This was soldiers' bad fortune. They were bad." Some of the little kids acted out these dramatic events too, which I thought was very funny and not a bit cute.

Most of the Melons' eyes grew enormous and one lady's face turned ghost white as if she might faint into the dirt. The orange-mustache man scrunched his face and another man flicked dirt from his shirt as if he was afraid that the circus camp was giving him a disease. The yellow tree–haired lady just shook her head sadly throughout the whole tour and made *tsk tsk* sounds. Obviously they'd never want to live here, which was fine by me.

The quiet couple seemed to be trying hard to understand things. They were looking into the Snake Lady's tree and looking closely at the Hairy Bear Boy's skeleton tent and looking at the fire circle where the mean soldiers had been eaten; they spoke quietly to each other as they held hands, and looked a little disturbed about the lost circus and people being smooshed.

They even tried to ask questions: "But what happened to the circus people? Where did they go? What happened to all the animals?"

I was the only one who understood. No Melons ever asked these questions, so I didn't even know what to say. It was a long story.

I didn't let the leftover kids act out anything from Old Lady Suri's best story: the story about how my dad, the Green Alligator Man, was in love with my mama, the Tallest Woman in the World with a Tail. Old Lady Suri said that my mama was so tall that nobody could even see her. Not really. You only saw her thick tree legs and the tip of her tail because her head was somewhere in the sky. Only special people could see her face; like me, when I carefully walked the line up through the trees and through the clouds as she smiled at me. And my dad could see her face, of course, when he climbed up her tree legs and put his scaly arms around her and kissed her nose.

The Melons never would've understood it anyway.

Old Lady Suri said that she understood everything because she'd been to the old circus at least a hundred times in her hundred-year-old life before it became haunted. She said that there were all sorts of other interesting circus animals and circus freaks. She just couldn't remember exactly because her brain was a bit blurry and slippery.

That's why, Auntie Moo always says, it's really hard to know what is true and what is not true about the old circus. But I know that everything's true.

Sister Baroo clapped her hands together, which meant that it was time for the leftover kids' real performance. It wasn't nearly as interesting as the old circus. Still, she'd made us practice at least twenty times. Toro started the show by standing on his head for ten whole minutes, and some of the little girls did a shy, giggly dance next to the fire circle. George did a funny act with a monkey on his shoulder. He said something to the monkey and the monkey screamed back and the foreigners laughed.

Then all of the leftover kids sang a very long, sad song about how terrible the war was and how it never stopped. Melons liked singing. Even though they couldn't understand a single word, they all smiled and clapped. I was supposed to be singing and I was supposed to be the final act too. Sister Baroo wanted me to recite an entire cracker box written in English. She wanted the Melons to see how smart we were.

But I had already snuck away.

No one noticed as I plucked the leftover snake off the foreigners' dinner plates, and hid the leftovers in the pocket of my special occasion dress. I escaped through the pig yard and climbed way up into the very tallest tree.

In my tree I could see everything, just like a circus star. They'd never find me.

Or . . . they wouldn't have found me if it hadn't been for George.

While George was singing, the monkey jumped off his shoulder, stole one of the Melons' purses, and dashed through the woods and straight up my tree.

"I FOUND HER!" shouted George. "And the monkey! And the purse!"

"Shhhhh! George, no!" I hissed down at him. My tree shook a little, and the monkey threw tree nuts down at George.

"HI, BABO!" George waved happily into the tree. "What are you doing up there?"

"Quiet, George!" I bugged my eye out at him. "Shhhhh."

I'd have to go higher to hide. But as I stood up, wobbly and shaky from my missing toes, George said: "Babo! Sister Baroo has been looking for you! One of the foreign couples wants to adopt an older girl. They want to talk to *you*, Babo."

I sucked in a bunch of air and nearly fell straight out of my tree. "Me?"

The Horrible Unhappy Promise

"THIS IS . . . MR. and Mrs. . . . Buck-worth. They come from . . . Amair—eek—a," Sister Baroo announced in her bad baby English. The quiet couple was politely sitting on a log in front of the elephant ring: the Buck-worths. I got to stare at them up close. The woman, Mrs. Buckworth, had nutty brown hair that was almost as short as a boy's. It curled under each ear like a baby pig's tail. Her teeth were cleaner than a row of river stones and her eyes were the color of sea-green water. Mr. Buckworth had thick tree legs and curly hair the color of a copper coin. He had eyes like George that twinkled as if he had a funny secret. Neither of them was elephant fat or skin-'n'-bones skinny, which was very unusual. The leftover kids always called me Big Mouth, but suddenly my words were eaten up. My knees were shaking. What are you supposed to say to a Melon?

Normally I hid until the Melons were gone, or I made funny faces so they'd think my brain was out of order. Sometimes I let my tongue hang out the side of my mouth like a lizard and they'd go away. But the Buckworths stayed.

This time I bugged out my fish eye so the Buckworths would think that I was really haunted, really broken, but they didn't even seem to notice.

"Can we call you 'Babo'?" asked Mrs. Buckworth. Her face was light brown from the sun.

I stared at her until Sister Baroo nudged me. She was still mad about the cracker box.

"Uh," I finally answered, "yes?"

"Babo, we just . . ." Mr. Buckworth put his elbows on his knees and spoke in a soft voice. "We want to know a little about you."

"What?" I scrunched my eyes. "Like what?"

"Well, what you love to do," continued Mr. Buckworth. He leaned forward and looked straight into my eyes, which made me very nervous. "The things you care about."

I shook my head so my hair would cover up my bad eye.

Mrs. Buckworth was tilting her head and waiting. "What makes you happy, Babo?"

I didn't answer. Instead, I looked up to where my line went into the sky and I imagined my mama, the Tallest Woman in the World with a Tail. She was waving and smiling down at me. My dad the Alligator Man was waiting at the bottom. He smiled too, and his green scales sparkled like water in the sun.

"I like the circus. I like to eat snake," I finally spit out. "That make me happy. I like to chase pig and get dirty. And play game. And get more dirty." My words were mushy as I searched my brain for the right ones. "I have Big Mouth. I tell Big Mouth stories. Sometimes scary stories. I like to go to the market. And I do not like Melons."

Sister Baroo flicked my back and I made a face.

"That's okay." Mr. Buckworth shook his head. "I don't like melons that much either."

Mrs. Buckworth laughed, and I swear her smile arched all the way up to her round Melon eyes. "We have one daughter," she told me. "Her name is Lucy. She's younger than you. And she really wanted to come here with us, to meet you and the other kids."

"She likes to play games too," added Mr. Buckworth. "And she likes to talk."

My ears perked up. "She has Big Mouth?"

Mr. Buckworth squeezed Mrs. Buckworth's knee. "Yeah, I guess you could say that." They laughed a private laugh. "You'd probably like her a lot, Babo."

I stared.

"We heard that you're so great with the little kids here," continued Mrs. Buckworth. "That you protect them."

I looked over my shoulder. The leftover kids were all watching like orangutans behind a thick tree.

"We also heard that you love to learn and you study very hard. Auntie Moo here tells us that you're very smart."

I whipped my head around and caught Auntie Moo's eyes. She looked down and pretended to sweep the fire circle.

"No!" I said loudly. "She is wrong. I mix words and make big trouble. Not smart."

Mr. Buckworth laughed. In fact, both of the Buckworths seemed to laugh all the time. This was not a bit funny. "Uh-oh," said Mr. Buckworth, "Lucy gets into big trouble too. Now with the two of you? At the same time? Well, Mrs. Buckworth and I are probably asking for a handful!"

I also didn't know how the Buckworths thought they were going to fit Lucy and me into their hands, unless Lucy had a teeny-tiny puppet head, but if they didn't care that we were big trouble, then I had to try even harder. I practically screamed, "I am very, very OLD. Foreigners do not adopt old children. They want babies. And pretty children. And I am not pretty!"

"Nonsense," said Mr. Buckworth. "You're such a beautiful girl."

"You really are, sweetie." Mrs. Buckworth put her hand on my bony chicken wing shoulder.

My face suddenly felt warm and I smiled, just a little, because I couldn't help it. "My mama is beautiful. Most beautiful woman in world."

"I'm sure you're right about that," agreed Mrs. Buckworth. "She must've been very beautiful too."

I pointed straight above the Buckworths' heads. "She live up there."

The Buckworths both looked up at the same time. "In that tree?" Mr. Buckworth squinted his eyes.

"No. In sky."

Mr. and Mrs. Buckworth nodded their heads, still peering into the hot sun, even though the sky was empty.

I wanted to change the subject. Fast. "What about *you*?" I asked them. "I want to know about you."

"Well, we do lots of fun things together," Mr. Buckworth started. "As a family."

"Like *what*?" I couldn't imagine Melons having any fun at all.

"We go bowling, and skating, and we go out for dinner—"

"And we go on vacations once in a while too," added Mrs. Buckworth. "You'd probably love that."

"Last year we went to Disneyland."

Whatever Diznee-land was I didn't love it at all.

The Buckworths were quiet and so was I, for once.

"Oh, you probably don't understand all of that, do you," said Mr. Buckworth.

"Are we talking way too fast?"

"Sorry, Babo."

Mrs. Buckworth started talking slowly, as if she had sweet potato mush stuck in her throat. "We heard . . . that you speak . . . excellent English, but—"

"I understand," I said quickly. "America is happy. You are happy. You love Diznee-land. Lucy has Big Mouth."

Auntie Moo gave me a sly look out of the corner of her eye. I still couldn't believe she had told the Melons anything good, anything at all, about ME.

"And my family live . . ." I folded my arms across my chest and stuck my nose in the air. "Here. Happy."

Mr. and Mrs. Buckworth gazed at each other before Mrs. Buckworth said, "Well, we really want to ask— if you think you could be happy in America too?"

"Would you like to—to come to America, Babo?"

The two of them, sitting on that log, looked awfully hopeful.

I poked at a rip in my special occasion dress and said, "America is too big. I will get lost."

Sister Baroo inhaled until I thought she was going to fall over, but the Buckworths just laughed.

"We wouldn't let you get lost, Babo," said Mr. Buck-worth.

"We promise." Mrs. Buckworth smiled.

But promises from Melons didn't mean much. Melons had promised to make our country better. They had promised to help us, not to steal us away.

The Buckworths kept talking and laughing and asking me things for a whole bunch of time. I knew I didn't give the right answers. I was trying to make the Buckworths choose another leftover kid, but as it turned out, they liked ME. It wasn't supposed to go like this at all.

How were my real mama and dad supposed to find me in America?

The Buckworths and a Boom

Soon I almost forgot about those Buckworth Melons and I was sure they forgot about me. They probably picked a pretty kid with two good eyes. They probably picked a kid who really wanted to go to America. Or a kid who didn't have a Big Mouth. Or a younger kid who could play with their puppet-head kid and wouldn't get into big trouble.

But a couple of months after their visit to the circus camp, Sister Baroo came running up the dirt path from the village. She was waving around an envelope.

Good luck or bad luck, it was hard to say. I thought it was probably very, very bad luck.

I didn't understand exactly how it happened, but the Buckworths called an agency in their country, and the agency mailed the thick envelope to Sister Baroo at the Mission, and the Buckworths wanted to adopt me.

It all happened way too fast. I'd be leaving for America in just two days.

The leftover kids squished into a huddle as Auntie Moo and Sister Baroo held out the pictures. In one picture, Mr. and Mrs. Buckworth stood smiling in front of a funny-looking tree. In another, a little girl was wearing red shoes with wheels on the bottom. Auntie Moo said that this was Lucy. My new little sister. She was missing her teeth, so Toro asked Auntie Moo if Lucy lost all her teeth in the war. Most of us were missing at least a few. But Auntie Moo said there was no war in America; Lucy's teeth fell out by themselves.

"Scary," said Toro.

"Why do they need me then, if they already have a kid?" I scrunched my face. It really didn't make any sense.

"Maybe they want another one," said George.

"They seem like very nice people, Babo," said Auntie Moo.

She had already told me about ten times that the Buckworths wanted me even though I was old. Melons usually think that older children are mean and angry, much more wounded from the war than the younger kids. Scarred from the inside out. But Old Lady Suri from the bean stand said that foreigners don't want to adopt older children because we're less likely to become Melons. Old children like me are stuck like bean paste to the ways of our real home.

"I have a good feeling about them," continued Auntie Moo. "I think you're going to like it there."

"I like it *here*," I said with my arms crossed and my nose high up in the air. But then I looked around and shut my Big Mouth. The leftover kids were looking at the pictures, oohing and aaahing. All of them wanted to be chosen by a Melon. All of them wanted to go to America. All of them except for me.

And then Auntie Moo told George that he was going to America too. We were going to live in the same village because the Buckworths' friend was going to adopt him. Our village in America was not the biggest village and not the smallest, but somewhere in between. We all leaned over to see the picture of George's new life. A young woman stood in front of a purple plastic thing filled with water. Auntie Moo said that the plastic thing was called a "swimming poo" and that children in America swam in it.

"Why will George have to swim in that weird little plastic thing?" I practically shouted. "Why can't he just swim in a river or a swamp like NORMAL kids?"

None of the leftover kids were paying any attention to me because they were too busy staring at the lady who was going to steal George away from the circus camp. She was smiling, and underneath the picture in very neat and pretty letters she had written: *I can't wait to see you, George.*

George stared at the picture too, and his eyes looked like they'd pop straight out of his head. "She's my mommy?"

"She'll be your adopted mommy, yes," laughed Auntie Moo.

George wouldn't let anyone hold the picture after that. He was afraid it would get chewed or torn up.

THE NEXT NIGHT, before George and I left on an airplane for America, we all sat in a circle in the lion cage. Auntie Moo put a bowl of peanuts in the center and sat down too. I had to tell one last important story . . .

"The beautiful girl was ready for her special show up in the sky. When she looked down at her audience the soldiers were there. Hundreds of soldiers. Mixed in with all the circus people. And those soldiers smiled and laughed—"

"What?" asked Toro, tugging on my shirt. "What's happening, Babo?"

I had to repeat every part of the story straight into Toro's ear because his hearing was messed up. I skipped over some parts fast and went on:

"But the soldiers were afraid of the beautiful circus girl because of her freaky eye. Just like they were

afraid of the other circus freaks. So she was chosen to go away—to a very foreign place—all because of those lousy soldiers and the lousy war."

"Some soldiers are very nice, Babo," said George.

"SHHH!" I swatted him. "So . . . *With her Big Mouth, the beautiful circus girl was definitely going to tell the foreign Melons all the mean stories about the war. Because they should know. But—"*

But just then, when I was getting to the good part, a huge explosion rocked the circus camp.

BOOM! BOOM! BOOM!

We shook and so did the lion cage. FLASH! The sky lit up with colors. Whites and reds. Gray smoke filled the air. BOOM! All of us hit the floor and covered our heads with our hands.

"Babo?" said George.

"Boom," said Toro.

"Children," whispered Auntie Moo. "Stay down."

Then there was another BOOM, even closer. We heard big boots running down in the village and lots of shouting. Soldiers were in the woods, not far from the pig yard. They were speaking gobbledygook words. It was impossible to tell where they came from and whether they liked us or not.

But there was only so long we could duck down without getting fidgety. We were way too used to big blasts and marching men and a smoky sky. George grabbed a handful of peanuts and crunched on them, which made Auntie Moo hold his hand and put her finger to her lips. Shhhh.

I was sick of being quiet. I was sick of everyone being so afraid.

"I'm not afraid of you," I whispered.

"Babo . . ."

I stood up in the lion cage and held on to the bars and whispered even louder, "I'm not afraid of you."

Toro whimpered, "Don't have a Big Mouth now, Babo," and a few of the leftover kids slapped their hands over their mouths. I could barely make out the white in their wide-open eyes. I didn't care. I was the brave one. I stomped out of the lion cage and stood alone at the base of the woods. "I'm not afraid. I won't be afraid!"

I knew that's what the circus people probably said, my mama and dad. They probably shouted it up to the sky. The earth probably shook like crazy as their voices echoed across my country and probably the whole world. "YOU CAN'T MAKE ME AFRAID!"

My voice came out smaller than a squeak. No one could hear me, not even the hairy spider on my foot.

BOOM! BOOM!

I dropped to the ground and covered my head.

I was a little afraid.

Auntie Moo walked to the entrance of the lion cage and called my name quietly, but I knew she couldn't see me in the dark. And she knew that I was way too stubborn about soldiers. If they were going to get anyone, they'd get me.

After half an hour, the soldiers moved on. Auntie Moo shook her head, as usual. "Come in now, Babo. Come back with us."

I mumbled, kicking my feet as I walked back to the lion cage.

We were all quiet until George whispered, "How does it end, Babo?"

"How does what end?"

"The story. The beautiful circus girl?"

"Well . . ." I took a deep breath. "She did have to go away. But she knew everything was going to be okay. Someday she would make it back, because the circus is her home."

My story made everyone feel sort of okay. Auntie Moo left to sleep by the fire circle and I waited until the last leftover kid fell asleep.

Then I stepped over them and left the lion cage. The logs from the fire were turning from red hot to black ash. Without even saying any words, Auntie Moo sat up and I crawled onto her lap, and she hugged me and we rocked back and forth. She didn't mind that I was about ten years old and way too big.

"Are you sure they'll like me?" I whispered. "The family?"

"Of course they will." Auntie Moo ran her fingers through my knotty hair. "Why wouldn't they?"

"Because one of my eyes is broken?"

"Babo, the Buckworths don't care about your broken eye. They like you exactly the way you are."

"Maybe. But what about the rest of those people in America? If they don't like me, well, how am I supposed to get back here?"

"Hmmmm." Auntie Moo thought about that. She straightened out her long braid and it brushed against my face. "It will be difficult. You're right about that."

I sniffled and squeezed my eye shut so I wouldn't cry. "Then how will I get to see you again, Auntie Moo?"

"I'll be right here, Babo. You can always write to me." Auntie Moo sighed. I listened to the sounds of the circus camp: an owl's hoot from far away, and a few lost birds calling to each other from the trees, and the frogs croaking by the river, and the leftover children talking in their sleep. "Sometimes things aren't as bad as we imagine, Babo. You're going to be okay."

I hid my face in Auntie Moo's chest, just like a baby, and she hugged me tighter. I breathed in Auntie Moo's special smell of fire and sweat and sweet potato. I knew I'd miss Auntie Moo forever and she'd miss me. But things were like that during a war. People were here, and then they were gone. Just like that.

"What is my new name again?"

"They're going to call you 'Betti,'" answered Auntie Moo. "It was Mrs. Buckworth's mama's name."

"Betti."

"It's a nice name, don't you think?"

"It doesn't sound right at all. No. It sounds weird."

Auntie Moo was quiet. "They thought it'd be easier for you to have an American name. It'll take some getting used to." She kissed the top of my head. "Having a new name doesn't mean you need to forget your old name, Babo. You'll have two names, that's all. And having two names is luckier than having just one."

"Really?" I took a deep breath. "Betti . . . and Babo. Babo . . . and—but Auntie Moo, you promise—"

"I promise, Babo."

"Tell me again. Please?"

"I promise if the circus comes back again, I'll tell them—your mama and dad—where you are. I promise." Auntie Moo's promises were always good.

So there were no words left in any language.

The Last Wave

"PSSST, BABO."

"Shhhh. Go back to sleep, George."

"Wake up! You have to wake up. It's the day." George touched my cheek with his hand.

I grumbled and put my potato sack over my face.

"The taxi's coming, Babo," whispered George. "I can hear it."

I wiped away the sleep from my eyes and looked around the lion cage at the leftover children. Dreaming. Crunched together in the corners like always. It wasn't fair.

A car was grumbling its way up the path from the village. It was shooting off noisy engine sounds: *Pow pow pow.*

I tied my orange bag that I had sewn all by myself.

There wasn't much inside: my potato sack, my pictures of the Buckworths, my old pair of pants and my shirt that was donated to Sister Baroo's Mission, and a jar of dirt from the circus camp. Best of all was the doll that the leftover kids had made for me. George got one too. They were made out of enormous donated foreign socks. The leftover kids had sewn strands of their hair at the top of the socks, and stuffed the socks with straw, and made strange-looking arms and legs with tied string. They had also painted faces on our socks with ash and red bean paste and pig sloppy slop. My doll was a girl with a good eye and a broken eye. George's doll only had one arm.

As for me? My present to the leftover kids was my Big Mouth stories. I'd made them repeat my stories over and over so they wouldn't forget. I quizzed them about the Tallest Woman in the World with a Tail, and the Alligator Man, and the clowns who all had red hair, and how the soldiers got eaten and smooshed.

I don't know if the leftover kids liked my present a bit, but I wanted them to remember. They had to remember.

I slipped on my new shoes. Sister Baroo had used her egg money to buy George and me plastic flip-flops so we wouldn't go barefoot on the plane. I was already wearing my circus dress to make me feel better on this horrible day.

George and I tiptoed over the leftover kids.

Then we leaped and skipped around the big "We Love You" that the leftover kids had taken two days to carve with stones and sticks into the circus camp dirt. They'd started as soon as George and I found out we were being taken away. It went across the fire circle, through the elephant ring, and all the way down to the ripped-up circus tents. But I was the only smart one who knew that George and I would never be able to see any "We Love You" from so high up in an airplane.

The taxi pulled up with a screech by the fire circle and puttered to a stop. Our taxi was an old dented Chevy. A driver was sitting in the front seat, chewing and spitting nuts that made his whole mouth red. When he opened his taxi door it fell off into the dirt. The driver cursed. Then he picked up the door and set it back in place and kicked it shut.

Sister Baroo paid the driver, who nodded all sorts of times. He told her that he was absolutely positive he knew his way to the airport. He picked up our bags and threw them into the backseat. The leftover kids were finally awake and they ran out of the lion cage and over to the taxi. They all scrambled in after our bags. None of us had ever been in a car before. We'd only chased them and tried to touch them as they zoomed down the dirt road by the market.

"Shoo!" cried the taxi driver.

But the leftover kids didn't want to shoo from the taxi. They were having too much fun playing with the big wheel in the front seat, and honking a horn that made a sick *achoo-achoo* sound, and putting their dirty hands all over the windows. The taxi driver got so upset that it looked like smoke was going to blow out of his ears.

"SHOO!" he cried again, waving his arms around. "Shoo, shoo!"

Auntie Moo had to pull the leftover kids out of the taxi, one by one. Then she put her soft, sundried arms around all of them as they hugged her wraparound skirt. George and I hugged Auntie Moo too, until the driver cleared his throat, which meant that it was time for us to go. We finally climbed into the backseat of the Chevy taxi. George and I both squeezed our dolls as the taxi driver kicked the door shut.

Sister Baroo, in her boring black dress, reached her hand through the window. She was waving around the last things that George and I needed: our airplane tickets and other papers she said were very important to get us into America. We stuffed them in the bottom of our bags. Sister Baroo pretended to have a bug in her eye, but I knew she was crying.

Our driver started his taxi with an old fork. He twisted it around and around until the taxi sputtered to a start. George and I looked at each other. Then we stared out the back window as everyone waved and hollered, "Good-bye! We love you! Good-bye!"

And . . . we started rolling.

Auntie Moo put up her hand in a wave, and I put my hand up against the back window. Our hands stayed just like that. The leftover kids jumped up and down, but soon their screams faded and they were just tiny bouncing dots. Auntie Moo's face got smaller too, until I couldn't even see her anymore. Her face was the last face I saw at the circus camp.

Red Teeth and Hot Spots

GEORGE KEPT WAVING out the back window even after the circus camp was long gone. He was still waving when the driver turned around from the front seat and smiled at us with crooked red teeth. "Call me Big Uncle," he said. "You need anything? Well, Big Uncle is right here." He turned his eyes back to the road and straightened the dusty cap on his head.

George and I stared at him and nodded. Big Uncle wasn't a bit big. He was quite short, actually, and skinnier than a scarecrow in a bean field.

Big Uncle drove us over potholes and ratty roads as we bounced up and down in the backseat. The Chevy taxi was old—very old—and George and I had to scoot around the metal springs that were sticking up through the torn seat. I kept hollering, "*Ow ow ow ow*," as I got poked, but George just laughed as if this was the most fun he'd ever had in his whole life.

"How far is it to the airport, Big Uncle?" asked George, bouncing higher.

Big Uncle spit out the cracked driver's-side window. "Not so far. Not far at all, little man."

But it sure seemed far to me. An hour in the beat-up taxi rolled into two hours. And three hours. And then I lost track. But I didn't care. I wasn't excited about the airport or the airplane *or* America. The longer the taxi ride, the better.

Big Uncle drove us through villages and farms and over mountains. Smoke hung over some villages like an umbrella, and small fires burned on the ground when there was nothing left to burn. Buildings were lopsided and drooping, about ready to tip over, while others looked perfectly cut in half.

"From the war, Babo?" asked George, with his nose straight up against the window. "From a bomb?"

I shrugged. To me it looked like an enormous giant had stomped its way through my whole country, squashing tiny buildings and tiny people. Stomp stomp.

The worst villages only had a few people left. They walked around with ashy faces and glassy eyes like circus animals that had dug themselves out of the ground. Our taxi could've driven over their toes and they wouldn't have noticed.

George's stomach started making growl noises, but he was always hungry, so that didn't mean much. Sister Baroo didn't give us food money because she said we'd get to eat all we wanted on the airplane. So George whispered, "Do you think Big Uncle might buy us something to eat, Babo?"

I knew that Big Uncle didn't even have enough money for himself to eat, so I didn't want to ask. Instead, George and I pretended that we were already Melons, fat and full, watching Big Uncle on the telee-vizion box. That made us laugh like crazy.

George dug his hand around in his blue bag and pulled out the picture of his new mommy and the swimming poo.

"Big Uncle? Do you want to see my mommy?" George stuck his hand into the front seat. He tried to put the picture in front of Big Uncle's eyes, and I was afraid that Big Uncle was going to drive off the road.

"Nice," said Big Uncle without really looking at George's mommy. "Real nice, little man." Big Uncle cleared his throat and coughed into a ratty hanky and shooed the picture away. George carefully wiped off the picture and laid it on his lap.

Big Uncle took his taxi job very seriously. Delays and detours made him irritated, which was too bad because the taxi ran into all sorts of delays and detours. George and I had to go to the bathroom three different times on the side of the road. Then Big Uncle swerved to one side and nearly hit a group of women washing clothes. George and I, and all the women, had to push Big Uncle and his taxi out of the mud. And then . . . Big Uncle hit an especially big hole in the road.

George and I heard a hissing, exploding POP. As the taxi stopped with a jolt, both of us ducked down in the backseat and covered our heads with our hands. We thought that someone shot the taxi. I peeked up to see if there was someone—a soldier—hiding behind a tree or a cow. Nothing.

Big Uncle cried and cursed at his tire. He spit and shook his head. He waved his fist and I would've sworn that Big Uncle and his popped tire were going to get into a fight. Fortunately Big Uncle had the brilliant idea of stuffing bubble gum and chewed red nut goo into the popped tire hole. That seemed to do the trick, at least for the moment.

Big Uncle also had to get out of the taxi and shoo away cows in the middle of the road. The next time he had to shoo away skinny chickens in the road. And then goats. And then a large circle of dirty street children playing marbles. "Shoo! Shoo!" called Big Uncle, waving his arms around. But the animals and the children didn't want to shoo for Big Uncle or his beat-up taxi.

So Big Uncle ordered George to get out and do the job. But George ended up petting all of the animals instead of shooing them, and he played marbles with the dirty children. The children cheered and climbed on George.

Big Uncle grumbled and tooted the taxi horn. The sound, tinier than a sick sneeze, came out—*achoo-achoo*—which made everybody laugh and made Big Uncle curse.

From then on, Big Uncle made me shoo everything out of the road.

The worst delay of all was when we ran into a "hot spot," as Big Uncle called it. Soldiers were fighting like crazy, so the taxi had to make a detour through four villages out of our way. Big Uncle said that we didn't want any old soldier thinking that we were traitors, fighting for the other side. Very dangerous.

"Do you think we'll miss our plane?" I whispered to Big Uncle as George and I ducked on the backseat floor.

"No worries, no worries," replied Big Uncle, clearing his scratchy throat.

I shrugged. I wasn't worried a single bit. I hoped we'd run into more cows and hot spots. But George was worried. "They'll wait for us, won't they, Big Uncle? The man who flies the airplane? They wouldn't leave for America without us. Would they?"

Big Uncle didn't answer. He just grunted and chewed more nuts, making crunch-crunch sounds.

Once we were out of the hot spot George talked and talked. I'd never heard him talk so much. I closed my eyes and pretended to fall into a deep sleep—for about five minutes—but George was way too noisy with all his talking.

"I hope we'll be next-door neighbors, Babo."

"Yes."

"And go to the same school too."

"That'd be just great."

"And play in the swimming poo after school?" George smiled hopefully.

"Sure," I sighed.

"And we'll probably be friends forever. Don't you think, Babo?"

"George, sit still. Aren't you tired?"

"How could I be tired? We're going to America. We're going to see our mommies!"

I didn't even have the energy to explain to George—again—that my mom was *not* Mrs. Buckworth. My real mom was the Tallest Woman in the World with a Tail. Definitely *not* a Melon.

Auntie Moo told me that George's real mom and dad had almost certainly been killed. That's what happens during a war. A foreign soldier found George and brought him to the charity hospital because his arm was lost. The soldier named him George and the name stuck. When George was better, the soldier held his hand and led him to the circus camp. George trusts Melons and I think it's all because of that foreign soldier.

He was about three and I was about six. None of us knew what happened because George never talked about it. But he smiled on that day, even with a missing arm.

Weird.

Big Uncle's bushy eyebrows arched up as he gave me a look in the rearview mirror. "Isn't it time for the little man to take a nap?"

Finally George got tired of talking and fell asleep on my lap. Big Uncle was quiet too. I was afraid that he'd fall asleep like George, so every once in a while I gave the back of the driver's seat a little poke.

We left the circus camp in the morning when the sun was coming up, and when the taxi pulled to a stop the sun was down.

"Taxi ride ends here," announced Big Uncle.

The Biggest Bird

GEORGE RUBBED HIS eyes and sat up. "Are we at my mommy's house, Babo?"

I tried to see out the window into the blackness. "George, we haven't even left our country."

"Oh. I thought maybe we drove to America instead."

Big Uncle cleared his throat and bugged out his eyes at me in the rearview mirror. That meant that George and I were supposed to get out. So I took George's hand and we crawled out of the backseat and out of the Chevy. We stood next to each other in the dark.

Big Uncle revved the beat-up taxi engine. He opened his door and shook our hands and said, "Good luck." Then he tried to close his door again three times and finally it stuck. Big Uncle drove away fast, shooting up rocks and dirt with his taxi tires.

I didn't see a single star and I didn't see a single airplane. I didn't see any buildings that looked like an airport and I didn't see a single excited person with packed bags ready to fly to America. Maybe the plane would be coming soon? Maybe we had to wait? We'd never seen an airplane up close, or an airport, so we didn't know exactly what we were waiting for.

But then lights flashed on and there it was. In a mountain of rubble, which used to be the airport, we saw the airplane with wings bigger than the biggest bird in the whole world.

GEORGE AND I had never been to another country. We'd never even been to another village. We'd never been in a Chevy taxi and we couldn't remember ever being alone for a whole day without Auntie Moo. So on this day? Well . . .

Airplane people helped us up the airplane stairs and took our tickets and sat us down in our perfectly clean, striped seats. The airplane people wore uniforms like soldiers, but theirs were perfectly blue with no wrinkles and no holes. They told George and me that some lady from the adoption agency was supposed to meet us and help us to America, but officials wouldn't let her into our country at the last second because it was too dangerous. "We'll help you, though," said one airplane man. He had a sunny smile, not at all like a soldier. "We'll take care of you, okay? Don't worry."

I was worried. The plane finally rumbled and I sucked in my breath. I could see the wheels leave the ground, the front wheels and then the back ones. We went up and up, as George covered his ears and the plane went straight into the sky. I thought I might throw up, while George laughed as if this was the most fun he'd ever had in his whole life.

He stared with his nose against the window and waved.

"Who are you waving to, George?"

"Maybe they can see us at the circus camp!"

"No. They can see the plane, but they can't see us and we can't see them. Remember?"

"But I see 'We Love You.'"

I practically climbed right over him so I could see out the window. Nothing but pure blackness and dark clouds. "There's nothing there, George. There's no 'We Love You.'"

"It's there, Babo. I see it. You don't see it?"

I stared and stared. Maybe it was there. My good eye started watering and playing tricks. We Love You. I wanted to see it, but George had better eyes than me.

He was still waving out the window an hour later when an airplane lady asked us if we wanted drinks.

"Does it cost money?" I asked her in English.

"No," she said with a sugar smile. "It's free."

George and I looked at each other. Free. George ordered a Coca-Cola, but I didn't order anything because I knew that nothing ever came for free.

When George's drink arrived, I looked at the lady suspiciously. Old Lady Suri at the bean stand said that foreign Melons could be very sneaky. But the airplane lady didn't ask for money and George sucked his Coca-Cola through a straw and made *mmmm mmmm* noises. So when she walked by again, I tugged on her arm and ordered three Coca-Colas. She laughed and brought me all three for free.

George smiled in his cute way at all the airplane Melons, so they brought him games to play, and crayons. They didn't bring me any because I covered my head with a blanket. Still, I could hear everything.

"Isn't he so cute?" they cooed to each other in English.

George drew a picture of a little stick boy holding hands with a big stick woman. Under the woman he wrote in his scribbly letters: "mommy." He wrote the word in English like Auntie Moo taught him, which just figured, because then all the Melons had to come look at his picture.

"Are you going to meet your new mommy?" one of them asked.

He nodded his head, way too shy to speak his bad

English. Then, of course, he had to pull out that swimming poo picture.

I snorted and covered my head again.

The plane ride to America took nineteen hours, on three different planes.

George didn't sleep at all. He stared out the window and smiled, even when it was black outside. And me? I went into a foggy sleep where people fell from planes, tires flew around on their own, mamas and dads with tails did twirls on the wings, and no one ever left my country.

It seemed like days of hiding under the airplane blanket. Sometimes the plane shook us up and down and muffled voices came out of the airplane ceiling. I tried to pretend I was still in the lion's cage, where booms seemed safer than airplanes.

After an extra-big clunk, I rummaged around in my orange bag for my circus doll. I found her and set her in my lap. But folded up under my doll, in a neat little square, I found something even better. I held it in my hand very very carefully. A letter . . . for me.

Dear Babo,

When you get this you will probably already be in America. My heart is so happy for you! You must keep your eyes open (even your broken eye) to see everything, so you can tell me about our world. I believe it is beautiful, Babo, and I hope you think so too.

Remember that a wise student, a student who tries very hard, also makes the best teacher. This will be you. Teach something and learn something every day in America.

I will miss you forever and always. Until we see each other again.

Love, Auntie Moo

P.S. Please don't worry about us. We will be okay. And also . . . try not to get into too much trouble, okay? The Buckworths seem very nice.

I SNIFFLED LIKE crazy and I couldn't even help it. My good eye got very cloudy until I closed it tight. I dug down deeper into my seat, but that's when George's finger touched my cheek.

"Babo! I think we're here!"

Sure enough, everything finally stopped. I peeked past the old people in the seats next to us. Outside, there was an enormous white building with rows of enormous windows. The airport. George's eyes lit up and all he could say was, "BABO! LOOK!"

I carefully folded Auntie Moo's letter again and hid

it at the very bottom of my orange bag—under my pictures of the Buckworths—so it would never get lost.

I couldn't believe we were still alive.

I couldn't believe we were in America.

I stepped on a plane on one side of the world and stepped off on the other.

My old world was like this: leftover children and jungle dirt, lion cages and circus stories, explosions in the woods and the soft lap of Auntie Moo. In my new world, I'd have to go to something named Diznee-land, I'd play Lucy games, I'd swim in a swimming poo, and the Buckworths would call themselves my mom and dad.

And . . . I'd be called Betti.

Foreign Goop

I HELD GEORGE'S hand and wouldn't let go. We were both shivering and it wasn't even cold. I could see them right away. Mrs. Buckworth smiled and waved. A tiny hand appeared from behind her, and the hand was attached to a girl with red hair.

Meanwhile, George spotted his new mommy from the picture. Their scene at the airport was like something out of an American "mooo-vee." I'd heard all about them from Old Lady Suri at the bean stand. This one was a love story. George took a step and stopped. George's mommy took a step and stopped. Then they both ran toward each other, like crazy people, and hugged. George's mommy cried, and George looked so happy that I thought he might explode. Or wet his pants, which he does sometimes.

As for me? I wasn't sure what to do.

I looked down at my flip-flops. My knees were shaking.

Then a little hand grabbed mine. It was the red-haired sister with no teeth. "Hi, Betti!" she said in an American baby voice, flinging her arms around my waist. "That's a funny dress! It's pretty, kind of."

I was still clutching my circus doll in my other hand. Lucy reached out to touch my doll and said, "She's kind of a funny doll, Betti!" I immediately smooshed my doll against my chest as a whole bunch of foreign faces surrounded me and started hugging me. "Hello, Betti! Hi, Betti! Welcome to America, Betti!"

Betti? No. It didn't sound right at all.

I thought I'd stop breathing. I thought I'd faint, face-first, onto the airport floor. Suddenly *I* was the foreigner.

And George was already lost.

"George!" I cried out as loud as I could, but my words were lost too in all the loud English. I bounced up and down hoping to spot his large ears. The Americans probably thought I was very excited to be in their country. "George!" I shouted louder. With my bony elbows I tried to poke through the wall of tall Melons. Their foreign smell made me dizzy.

So I dropped straight to the floor. I threw my orange bag over my shoulder and held on to my circus doll by her leg and dragged her behind me. I crawled and crawled through the rubble of big shoes, and finally I spotted those dirty little feet. I clutched his flip-flop and held on. George wiggled his foot as if I was a snake.

"Hi Babo! What are you doing on the floor?" George said in our language. He giggled as he squatted down and tried to dust the dirt off my doll.

"George, don't scare me like that. You're going to get lost!"

"I'm not lost, Babo. I'm right here."

"I told you a hundred times. You need to be very careful in America. You need to be on the lookout at all times. You need to—"

"Are you two all right?" Mrs. Buckworth was suddenly squatting on the floor next to us.

"Very big feet here," I answered. "Very funny smell."

Mrs. Buckworth put her hand on my shoulder. "I know this all must seem so crazy."

"No crazy," said George.

I looked up and squinted my eyes. "I will maybe get squashed. I will maybe get stolen."

"Babo scared," said George.

I elbowed him. "I am NOT scared."

"Ohhhh," said Mrs. Buckworth. She put her arms around me like I was her baby. My face was touching her purple jacket and her neck smelled like Melon. "It's okay, Betti. I'd be scared if I were you," said Mrs. Buckworth. "I really would. Just stick with me, okay?"

I wasn't sure I wanted to be *stuck* to Mrs. Buckworth—she was a Melon and I hardly knew her—but I did want to squat with her there on the airport floor for a long long time; it was quieter, like being under a tent. But Mrs. Buckworth took my hand so she wouldn't be scared, and I tugged on George's hand, and the three of us stood up together so things wouldn't seem crazy. We were led along in a wave of towering tall people. I couldn't let George get lost again.

We rode down on stairs that moved and I was absolutely sure my feet would get sucked inside. I didn't want to lose more toes.

"George, are you scared now?" I asked, clinging to him.

"Why would I be scared, Babo? This is fun!"

I was supposed to be the brave one because I was the leader. But George asked his new mommy if he could ride up and down the moving stairs again and she let him do it three times. He laughed and squealed as we all waited. Everyone always loves George.

I kept whispering last-second things into George's big ear.

"If it's too horrible living with the Melon, you come and find me, okay? Just try not to get lost. And I know you're not going to be able to sleep for a while, you'll miss my stories before bed, but—"

"Babo." George tilted his head and looked at me. "Maybe my mommy will tell me a story before bed. Maybe I can ask her."

"But you won't understand her, George! She'll just say a bunch of foreign goop!"

Then George's new mommy hugged him for about the tenth time. I heard her trying to speak words in our language. She sounded like a four-year-old baby, and George answered in English like a four-year-old baby. They were a perfect, out-of-order match.

"Bye, Babo!" George yawned and waved. "I hope I get to see you really soon!"

Then all I saw was George's back, walking away from me with his mommy.

George is weird, but he's the only one who understands everything.

"Betti?" Mrs. Buckworth touched my shoulder and I jumped. She put her arm around me, and red-haired Lucy reached for my free hand. Mr. Buckworth gently took my bag from me—my whole life in an orange bag—and carried it over his shoulder like a sack of potatoes. Standing in front of us like scary glass soldiers were the airport doors that opened out into the world of America. That's when Mrs. Buckworth asked, "Are you ready to go home, sweetie?"

"Yes," I said. All I could think about was running like crazy and jumping back on that big bird airplane. "Yes. Home."

Home Sweet Melon Home

HOME IS A weird thing.

We rode in a long brown car that Mrs. Buckworth called "the wagon." It didn't look like any wagon I'd ever seen. Or like Big Uncle's taxi. I sat in the back next to Lucy as cars zoomed by us from every side. I wasn't sure if the Melon cars were all zooming away from some dangerous hot spot, or if they were zooming toward something very important in the center of their market.

Either way, I was right about America. Way too big. A leftover kid could get lost in about one second. I squinted my eyes and looked up at the sky; the tops of tall buildings disappeared in the clouds. On the ground everything looked way too clean. No dirt, no smoke, and I wondered where they had hidden all their trees and monkeys and soldiers.

The Buckworths started asking me questions but I was very busy, with my nose against the window, staring at their huge shiny village.

Mr. Buckworth's copper coin eyes looked at me from the mirror in the front seat. "So what did you think about the airplane, Betti?"

I gave his seat a little poke so he'd keep his eyes on the zooming cars. Then I held my arms out like enormous wings. "It was very bigger than a big, big bird. It fly."

Lucy scrunched her eyes. "You've *never* been in an airplane before, Betti?"

I shook my head. "George and me think it fly away already. Because Big Uncle's taxi too slow. Cows and houses fall down and kids are dirty and hot spots . . . We did *not* want to be traitors. But the airplane wait for George and me. In a mountain. Of rocks."

"I've been on an airplane so many times," said Lucy. "Never in a mountain of rocks, though. I flew to Florida once and I saw Mickey Mouse and there was this show where all these kids were singing and—"

"George and me have Coca-Cola for free," I said.

"Everybody gets free Cokes, you silly." Lucy touched my knee with her little finger.

Lucy had a big mouth. But my mouth was bigger. "*Then*, I see 'We Love You' on the ground. Little pigs . . . kids . . . at circus wave like Coca-Colas . . . I mean flags . . . so I open window." I waved my arms around like crazy for effect. "I climb out on airplane bird wing and walk careful on my line so I do not fall. Then I wave too. And I dance like the circus. 'We love you,' they scream. 'We love you.' And the ghosts on the airplane say, 'We love you' too. They tell me to go back home."

Lucy scrunched her eyes. *"What?"*

"Luce, why don't you let Betti relax for a few minutes," chuckled Mr. Buckworth. "She just had a very long trip."

"I know, Dad, but I'm trying to understand like you said." Lucy wiped her nose and sighed. "But Betti's talking about dancing ghosts and you said there aren't any ghosts. And she's talking about some waving circus pigs and Coca-Cola. I don't really understand what she's talking about, Dad. Not a bit." She turned and stared at me. I was a freaky animal in a zoo.

That's when I ducked my head down and covered my eyes with my circus doll.

And I didn't even peek out the window until the wagon finally stopped zooming and slowed down.

There was a whole long line of houses, but the house I liked the most was one that looked just a little tilted. So I tilted my head too and rubbed my good eye. There was a girl reading a book on the tilted porch. She had bushy brown knotty hair that covered her head like a wooden bowl. Wild hair, as if it hadn't been combed in weeks. If she hadn't been a Melon, I might've thought she was a circus girl. I watched her out the back window until her house disappeared, and so did she.

Soon the wagon stopped in front of a sky blue house. It was square with a real roof that wasn't caved in. It had windows that weren't shot out and exotic foreign flowers that hung in pots like pretty birds in stringy nests.

Not a fancy royal palace at all, like Old Lady Suri at the bean stand told me. She said that everyone in America lived in houses practically bigger than our whole village. She had seen it herself on a tele-veezion when she went to visit her sister in the capital.

She said that every house had a hundred rooms so no one ever saw each other. When they *did* see each other, well, it was either a dramatic love story or a horrible tragedy. Either way, the Americans were crying all the time.

Auntie Moo told me not to believe everything I heard at the market. "Most Americans don't live like that, Babo," she said. "Most Americans are like you and me. They just happen to be living somewhere else." Still, Auntie Moo had never seen a tele-veezion box like Old Lady Suri.

But when Lucy jumped out of the wagon, and Mrs. Buckworth grabbed my orange bag, and Mr. Buckworth opened my wagon door, I thought that maybe Auntie

Moo was right. At least about the Melons' houses. The Buckworths' house was pretty, very pretty, and a whole lot bigger than the lion cage, but it definitely didn't have a hundred rooms. I was glad. It sounded awfully lonely getting lost in a hundred rooms with Melon ghosts flying around.

"This is it," said Mr. Buckworth as he picked me up in his hairy bear arms. "Home sweet home."

And that's when the tour of my new life started.

WELCOME BETTI!

Big lopsided letters were draped across the whole room when I walked inside.

There were also colorful balls hanging from the ceiling. "Balloons!" cried Lucy. She poked one and it exploded and I nearly flew out of my flip-flops.

"I made that myself!" Lucy pointed at the banner, which looked very useful for scaring off hungry scavengers from the bean fields. "Now come on, Betti! I wanna show you *everything*!" Lucy grabbed my hand and started pointing at all sorts of other things.

Mikroo-wave.

It makes things really hot really fast.

Lucy pushed a button. Ding.

I looked on top of it and underneath it and behind it. No waves at all. No firewood. Not even a teeny red spark of fire. Weird.

Ree-frigger-ater.

"For food," said Mrs. Buckworth.

Ree-frigger-ater is cold. Stove. To cook food.

"It's hot, Betti. Never touch the stove when it's hot."

Cold. Hot.

Kichin. Dineeng Rooom. Bath Rooom. The Living Rooom had funny painted pictures hanging on the walls. And funny pictures of a baby with red hair. And then . . . I saw it! It looked exactly like Old Lady Suri said. A huge tele-veezion staring out from the wall! My good eye got big.

"TV," said Lucy pointing at the tele-veezion.

"TV?" I repeated.

She pushed a button in her hand and the tele-veezion magically came alive. I jumped back and gasped. I was afraid to move. There were two real live people talking to each other on the tele-veezion TV!

Lucy giggled. "You've never seen a TV, Betti?"

I shook my head. My knees were shaking too.

Lucy pushed the button over and over—flash flash flash—and the magic TV flashed with new people every second. The trapped TV people must've done something very horrible. That's when Mrs. Buckworth came into the living room and took the thing out of Lucy's hand and made the TV people disappear. The box turned black.

"No TV right now, Lucy," said Mrs. Buckworth.

"Maybe you can show Betti some TV later. Maybe tomorrow."

Lucy's lip jutted out for about a second, but then she ran to another door and swung it open. "BASEMENT!"

Base Mint? Mint was green and cured hiccups and hives.

But this was no plant. It was a huge black dog that suddenly appeared and leaped right over to me!

"DOG!" shouted Lucy as she laughed and barked.

"DOG!" I screamed back and jumped on top of one of the fluffy chairs. My heart practically flew right out of my chest.

"Sit, Rooney!" hollered Lucy. But Rooney didn't want to sit. He wanted to stare at me with his mouth open and his black tail flying back and forth. Big teeth and bad breath.

Lucy climbed on his back. "Giddyup! Giddyup!" She kissed his runny nose.

Mr. Buckworth held on to Rooney by a purple thing around his neck. Then Mr. Buckworth held out his other hand and helped me down from the chair. "Don't worry, Betti," he said in a voice that was way too calm. "He's a nice dog."

I wasn't sure about that. Not sure at all.

In *my* village, I always ran away from packs of tired, hungry dogs. Once, I hid for an hour, but a leftover dog had waited and peed on me like I was a tree.

But I had to be nice to the fat American dog, or the Buckworths would make me disappear in their TV box or their microwave. That's when Mrs. Buckworth told us to sit at the eating table. Rooney licked my missing toes under the table and I tried not to scream.

"Spaghetti," announced Lucy. "Dad made it."

"Spooogetti," I repeated. It turned out that spaghetti was a big bowl of snakes. I didn't know that Melons ate snakes too, even though Mr. and Mrs. Buckworth ate our snake at the circus camp.

I picked one up with my finger and stared at it up close. "Skinny," I said. "No eyes and no mouth."

Lucy giggled and licked her lips. "Yummy," she said, which must've been the word for thanking the snakes for letting us eat them.

I grabbed a whole pile of skinny blind snakes in my hands. I chewed and slurped until my plate was empty. "Yummy," I said.

Mrs. Buckworth smiled and gave me more. I didn't tell Mrs. Buckworth that I'd already eaten three different meals on three different airplanes. But I kept eating snakes, and more snakes, until the Buckworths all stopped eating at the same time.

Mrs. Buckworth looked a little worried. "Um, Betti? You must be so hungry! But there's plenty of spaghetti, okay?"

Lucy started to laugh like crazy and picked up a pile

of snakes with her little fingers. She stuffed a whole handful in her mouth.

I was supposed to eat my spaghetti snakes with a fork. That's what Mrs. Buckworth said, and she showed me how. I'd seen forks used for all sorts of things, like starting taxis, but never for eating. Forks really didn't make much sense; it was much easier to eat with my fingers because my snakes kept slithering off my fork.

Mr. Buckworth pushed his plate aside and put his elbows on the table so he could stare at me extra close. "We're so happy you're finally here, Betti."

Lucy bounced in her chair as if she had baby mice trapped in her pants. "Especially me. I couldn't wait. If I had to wait another day I was gonna die."

I set my fork down and stopped chewing. Lucy was going to die? I gulped.

"It'll take some time for you to get used to being here," said Mrs. Buckworth in her soft voice. "America is so different."

"Your country's kind of scary," said Lucy. "And poor."

"Lucy."

Lucy shrugged.

"But we've been trying to learn about your country too. So we can understand. Haven't we, Luce. Let's show Betti the book."

Lucy ran to the living room and grabbed an enormous book that sat by itself in the middle of a glass table. "Here." She held it out to me.

I turned the pages of the book slowly, while the Buckworths huddled around me. The three of them looked at each picture and then looked at me.

The Buckworths must've thought that I was some sort of expert on my whole country. They must've thought that I loved their big book, because soon I started flipping fast through all the pictures until I got to the very end. Actually I was just looking for pictures of Auntie Moo or the leftover kids or the tallest lady in the whole world with a tail.

Nothing.

The shiny pictures must've been taken before the war, a long, long time ago.

"Your country is pretty, Betti," said Lucy, leaning right against me so her cheek touched mine.

I nodded. "My trees are pretty. My animals are pretty. I climb better than monkeys. Sela was pretty one. She got adopted because she is pretty. Curls and eyes. Other leftover kids inside pretty. That's what Auntie Moo say. Not pretty like Sela, but very pretty on inside.

"This book . . ." I sadly shook my head. "People have fingers. And toes. No circus people. No hot spots. No houses like broken bones. No pretty on inside people."

My good eye started to tear up. I sniffled a little and

closed my eye tight like I had a bug in it, even though there were no bugs in the Buckworths' house. "I think this country is . . ." I closed their big book. "Not my country."

Moms and Mermaids

BED ROOOM.

Square and yellow. Almost as big as the lion cage. Auntie Moo and all the leftover kids could have slept in it, even though Lucy said it was all mine. But I wasn't going to like it a bit because I wasn't going to be at the Buckworths' house for long.

After dinner, when Lucy showed me my new bedroom, I peeked out a window and saw the sky turning dark blue and black. I squinted and saw a perfect square of real grass. Old Lady Suri said that my village used to have real grass too, until the soldiers stomped the grass down to nothing with their brown boots. An arched metal thing stood in the center of the Buckworths' grass with two hanging empty seats.

"Your window looks at the backyard and mine looks

at the front. My room's right there, see?" Lucy pointed to an open door across the hall. A pink room. "But maybe Mom'll let us have slumber parties and I can sleep in your room. In a sleeping bag."

Then Lucy pointed to something on my bed. It was the best thing in my whole room! "He's for you. He's so cute, don't you think?" Lucy picked up a stuffed bear that had a red ribbon around his neck. She kissed its black plastic nose.

I reached out to touch its fuzzy fur. Its wide-open eyes stared back at me and his thready mouth smiled.

"I picked him out myself!"

It was a CIRCUS BEAR, kind of, even though it was fake. So I pulled my circus doll out of my orange bag and dusted her off. I set her carefully on my bed next to my circus bear.

Sometimes Melons donated boring white socks that we never wore and soapy teeth paste to the leftover kids, but I'd never been given a present that was just for me. "Thank . . . you," I said, just as Auntie Moo had taught me to say when the Buckworths did something nice.

Lucy started bouncing up and down on my new bed, which made me very dizzy. "My mom said that your eye got hurt."

"Yes." I shrugged. I carefully pulled my jar of circus dirt out of my orange bag and set it down on a little table next to the bed. "It got broken."

"But how did it break?"

I was too tired to explain how my eye got lost in the war or the circus, so instead I said, "Ghost named Hairy Bear Boy tell me my fortune. He say I have to go to America. Good luck or bad luck, it is hard to say. Next day I wake up and my eye falls out. And my hair. And my toes fall off too."

Lucy's eyes grew huge. "Did he use a magic potion?"

"Yes, he did," I said dramatically. I wasn't sure what a magic lotion was, but I was sure that the Hairy Bear Boy must've used it.

Lucy tilted her head and plopped down on my bed. She scrunched her forehead. "But you're not bald now, and your eye is still here, sort of, and most of your toes—"

"They growed back." I laid my everyday pants from the circus camp at the bottom of my bed. "They just growed back funny."

"I wish I had an eye like yours, Betti." Lucy looked up at my fish eye as if she was looking at a funny painting. "Last year . . . mermaid . . . for Halloween . . . do you have Halloween, Betti?"

I had no idea what a halloweenie was, and I hoped I'd never had it.

Lucy swirled her finger around on her face, and up past her eyes. "Mom let me wear . . . makeup . . . my eyes. Blue . . ."

I could understand most of Lucy's Big Mouth words, but others were plain gobbledygook.

"But Mom says . . . no makeup 'til . . . I'm really old. Ninth grade . . . Only Halloween . . ."

"What does it mean? Merrrr-Made?" I asked.

"Mermaid? It's a half girl, half fish. She has a tail and she's the same color as the ocean."

"She . . . swim?"

"She has to. She doesn't have any legs. A mermaid only has a tail."

Mermaid. I thought about all the people who floated away from my village. They were all probably mermaids by now, waving their tails at the bottom of the sea.

"Lucy!"

The Buckworths loved to scream back and forth to each other. Maybe their ears were out of order.

"Shhhh!" whispered Lucy as she put her little finger to her lips. "My mom wants us to go to sleep. But now that you're finally here I don't wanna go to sleep. Do you? We have so many things to do! You're going to play dolls with me and watch cartoons and we can roller-skate . . . For HOURS."

Suddenly I was very, very tired. I lay down on my bed and put my head on my very own "peee-lo." It was way too fluffy, but I was so tired that I could've slept on top of ten monkeys. I reached for my orange bag on the floor, took out my potato sack, and laid it carefully over that weird pillow.

Lucy lay down with her head next to mine. She closed her eyes. "Shhhh. We have to act like we're asleep." She reached out and softly closed my good eye for me, when . . .

Mrs. Buckworth walked into the yellow room.

Lucy let out a loud noise like a sleeping cow. She elbowed me, so I let out a cow noise too.

"Girls," laughed Mrs. Buckworth, "you can't fool me. Go put on your pajamas, Lucy, and then it's off to bed."

"Ohhhhhhh, Mom." Lucy bounced off my bed and ran out of my room. She was back in about one second. "Can we have a cookie first?"

"Tomorrow." Mrs. Buckworth sighed. "Now it's pajamas."

"Pajamas. I know." Lucy ran away again.

Mrs. Buckworth sat down on my bed and smoothed out my blanket with her hand. "Betti, I have some pajamas for you too."

"What is pujamuzz?" I asked.

She opened a secret drawer that was inside of a large wooden chest against the wall. She took out a long, fuzzy pink dress and held it up. "I wanted you to have something to wear tonight. I also bought some other things." She opened another drawer and then another. "I hope you like them."

Four pairs of pants, three pairs of shorts, eight pairs of socks and underwear, another striped pajamas dress, a "swimming soot for swimming in a swimming poo," and a pair of "overallzz." The overalls were blue and looked like what the poor farm people wore in my country. But mine had a red flower on the front.

Then Mrs. Buckworth walked to a skinny secret door and opened it. I curiously followed her and looked inside. Hanging like empty people from a pole that went from one side to the other, were three brand-new dresses and three brand-new shirts.

"And some shoes, Betti."

"Shoes?"

There were perfectly white shoes for playing, which I planned to get very dirty, and shoes kind of like my flip-flops, only fancier, with holes in the front that would show off my missing toes.

I looked down at my flip-flops. Sister Baroo had spent a lot of money for my flip-flops. They were just fine, but not here I guess, and yesterday seemed like a million years ago.

Then Mrs. Buckworth held up a third pair of shoes. "These are for birthday parties and special things like that."

Special occasion shoes! Red and shiny with buckles. My good eye bugged out and my mouth hung open. I wanted to touch all of my new clothes and my new red shoes. Instead I said, "Thank . . . you," and closed the door. I was not going to like any of it.

"I'll help you put on your pajamas, sweetie," said Mrs. Buckworth, "but first you can take a bath."

"Bath?" I said. I definitely didn't want my skin scrubbed until I was blue and raw and wrinkled like a baby elephant.

"I know you're probably so tired after your trip, but it might feel good to—"

"No bath, no bath." I put my arms across my chest. I pointed my nose at the ceiling.

"Oh. Well . . ." Mrs. Buckworth put her hand on my shoulder, on my circus dress. "I guess it can wait until tomorrow. Sure."

So I shyly let her help me put on my pajamas. My new pink pajama dress was soft and warm.

I sat down on my bed again. I yawned.

"Betti, I also wanted to give you this." Mrs. Buckworth handed me a book.

She watched hopefully as I was very busy flipping through the pages. I was afraid it was another book about my country that was not really my country. "It is no words," I said.

Mrs. Buckworth laughed. "It's a blank book. It isn't supposed to have words yet."

"Blank?"

"It's . . ." Mrs. Buckworth looked at the ceiling and itched her chin. "It's . . . empty. So you can write in it or draw pictures, whatever you want. Maybe you can write new English words in it so you don't forget them."

"M Tea." I itched my chin too. "My M Tea Book." I had no idea what Melon tea had to do with a book. But then Mrs. B. wrote the word on her hand: Empty. "My Empty Book," I said, and Mrs. Buckworth smiled. It had a purple cover with pictures of flowers and a smiling girl. And there was a blue pencil that was attached to it with a pink thing on the end. The pink thing looked like a little piece of candy so I bit it. Definitely not candy. I spit that thing on the floor.

Still, I loved my Empty Book! "Thank . . . you, Mrs. Buckworth," I finally said.

"You're welcome, Betti. It might be nice for you to have it. I mean, so you can look back on it someday. After you've been here for a long time."

A long time? I definitely wasn't going to be here for a long time. But I'd write everything in my Empty Book so I could show Auntie Moo about the world of America. Pictures that I'd drawn of my very interesting vacation here and all of my new words. I'd show Old Lady Suri at the bean stand and I'd show the leftover kids who would ooooh and ahhhhh, and best of all, I'd give it to my mama and dad when they came home to the circus camp.

Mr. Buckworth knocked softly on my bedroom door and walked in. Both of them sat down on my bed next to me.

"This . . ." Mr. Buckworth waved his hand around the yellow room. "This must all seem so new and strange, Betti."

I nodded. Very strange.

"But you don't have to feel shy. This is your home now."

The Buckworths were okay. Mrs. Buckworth gave me an Empty Book and red buckle shoes and she squatted with me on the airport floor. Mr. Buckworth made me spaghetti snakes and saved me from the Melon dog. Lucy taught me important words like "yummy" and "mikroo-wave" and gave me a stuffed hairy bear. In fact, the Buckworths were nice. For Melons. I played with my fingers and set my circus doll in my lap. It was all very confusing.

"I do not . . . understand," I said, trying to run my fingers through my doll's knotty leftover kid hair.

"What is it, sweetie?"

"I do not understand why you choose . . . me."

"Oh, Betti." Mr. Buckworth smiled and plunked his hand down on my head. "We knew we were going to adopt you when we first saw you."

"But . . . why?" I bugged out my eyes. "Did the ghosts tell you?"

Mr. Buckworth chuckled. "No. No ghosts. We just felt that you had so much courage. Like a little tiger."

I didn't know what "courage" meant, but I liked being a little tiger.

"And you're funny, Betti. We knew that Lucy would love you too," added Mrs. Buckworth. "That you'd teach her so many important things."

I thought about how I made the leftover kids memorize my scary Big Mouth stories. I thought about how I taught them all of my games that got us into big trouble.

"Auntie Moo say . . ." My good eye started to get cloudy, so I shut it tight. "Learn something and teach something every day in whole short life." I squished my circus doll against my chest, and wished that Auntie Moo were hugging me.

"Auntie Moo is smart, just like you." Mrs. Buckworth looked at me with kind eyes until I looked down. "We know you're going to miss her, Betti. And the other kids. That part's not going to be easy. You can talk to us about that too, okay?"

It wasn't supposed to go like this at all.

Somehow I'd have to make the Buckworths realize that I was definitely the wrong choice. Broken from the inside out. Somehow I'd have to get the Buckworths to throw me away, back to the circus camp, so they could get a new leftover kid. Not smart and not funny and not a little tiger, like me. I was going to have to be bad. *Really really bad.*

"We hope you'll feel happy here, Betti."

"Yes, Mrs. Buckworth."

Mrs. Buckworth's face turned pink. "You don't have to call us 'Mr. and Mrs. Buckworth,'" she said, brushing hair out of my eyes. "You can call us 'Mom and Dad.' I mean, if you . . . want to."

I thought about that. Very quietly I answered, "Okay, Mrs. Buckworth. And Mr. Buckworth."

The Buckworths slowly nodded their heads—Mrs. Buckworth looked a little sad—and they both bent over and kissed my forehead, just like Auntie Moo always did.

"Goodnight, Betti," Mrs. Buckworth whispered. "I hope you have sweet dreams."

I watched them tiptoe out of my yellow room.

If they hadn't chosen me I never would've been in this confusing mess.

I got up and took off my fuzzy pajamas and put on my circus dress. Only Melons wore pajamas. Then I dug around in my orange bag and found my letter from Auntie Moo, underneath my pictures of the Buckworths. I stuck it in the back of my Empty Book, and slipped my Empty Book under my pillow.

In front of my nose, next to my pillow, I propped up my fake circus bear and my circus doll.

"*My mama,*" I whispered to them both in my real language, "*is the Tallest Woman in the World with a*

Tail. She takes my hand and we dive in and out of the water. Mermaids. We can swim around for HOURS, because there is a whole country inside the purple plastic swimming poo. A whole country of watery circus people."

My bear and my doll were listening carefully. Their eyes were wide open.

"You can live there too, if you want to." I touched the circus bear's nose. "See, we are very safe, because no one knows about the country but us."

Eggs and Drool

IT WAS MY second day in America, and . . .

I opened my eye and screamed.

Something furry was staring at me. I didn't move.
I wasn't going to move because that's when animals
chase you. My potato sack was under my head. My circus camp doll was under one arm and my circus bear
was under the other. My special occasion dress was all
wrinkled, and my flip-flops were on my feet in case I
suddenly had to run. And the enormous furry black
thing started to wag.

Rooney.

"Shoo!" I hissed in my language as a big string of
drool fell out of his mouth and landed on my ear. He
opened his mouth wider. I was sure he'd bite my head
or lift his leg.

We were both underneath a tree next to the empty swinging seats. Rooney the American dog had followed me and slept outside with me. I could smell the grass and hear the birds and a bug crawled across my hand.

Then Rooney's huge slobbery red tongue lapped out and licked my bad eye!

"Help!" I screamed. This was the last word Auntie Moo taught me before I left in the beat-up taxi. She said I only needed to use it if I got into big trouble. "HELP! HELP!"

Suddenly Mr. Buckworth was sprinting through the backyard in his underpants.

"Betti! Are you okay? What are you doing outside?"

"P-pig," I stammered, pointing at Rooney. "Mikroo Wave Base Mint TV."

I meant to say "dog," but these were the words that came out. Even though Old Lady Suri said I'd get in big trouble for saying the wrong words, it really didn't matter at a time like this.

"Come on, boy," Mr. Buckworth said in a deep voice, so Rooney sat down and licked Mr. Buckworth's foot. Then Mrs. Buckworth ran outside, followed by Lucy.

Mrs. Buckworth tilted her head and said in a very worried voice, "Betti?"

"I . . . I . . ." I didn't have the right words. The Buckworths probably couldn't understand why I was sleeping outside. Maybe they just thought I loved nature or their swinging seats. "No kids . . . smooshed." I pointed to a corner of the fence as if it were the lion cage. "No George." I split my legs like a wishbone. "It is too very dark in there." I pointed at their sky blue house. "I cannot see."

I didn't know how to tell them that in the middle of my first night in America I woke up shaking and sweating in my new yellow room. I waved my arm back and forth to touch a leftover kid, or George's feet, but I couldn't find either one. I was all by myself and the Buckworths' house was way too quiet. It was definitely much safer outside.

I couldn't explain in English how it was very important to see straight up to the sky so I always knew if something was coming.

I raised my hands up. "Boom."

MRS. BUCKWORTH'S HAND set down a pretty plate right in front of me at the eating table. Clink. Bright yellow egg, circled by white goo. I poked the egg with my finger. Yellow goo spread across my plate and ran into cooked bread. This . . . was my first breakfast on my first day at the Buckworths'.

Scary.

Lucy bounced in her chair and made egg designs on her plate. "Look, Betti!" She kept grinning at me like a crazy red-haired clown. "Look at my egg."

"Eat your breakfast," Mrs. Buckworth told Lucy from one end of the eating table.

"Ick." Lucy stabbed her fork into her egg.

I made egg designs like Lucy. "Ick," I mumbled, which must've been the Melons' word for promising the ghosts that I wouldn't get into trouble, so they'd give me more food. I swirled my fork around and around on my plate. "Ick," I said politely to the ceiling.

I ate eggs in my country, but never eggs like this. Sometimes I climbed into trees and found polka-dotted eggs, and blue eggs, and yellow eggs. White eggs were the most boring of all. The Buckworths' cooked bread was boring too.

"It's called toast, Betti." Lucy jumped out of her chair. "Come here! Look!" She pushed a button on a white square box and waited. I peeked inside and suddenly the cooked bread magically popped up and nearly hit my nose. Lucy thought that was very very funny. "See?"

I didn't know why Melons called cooked bread "toes" but I got to make it three times by myself. Then Lucy showed me the red stuff that I got to squirt on my cooked bread. It oozed out in a big funny blob.

"Jelly," said Lucy with red teeth almost like Big Uncle's red teeth.

"Jellllly."

And I didn't really know what "break" meant, but I knew what "fast" meant, so I tried to eat as fast as I could. I dipped my fingers in the yellow goo and licked them fast. Goo dripped onto my plate and covered my lips. I stuffed cooked bread toes in my mouth fast, even though my cheeks puffed out.

Mr. Buckworth looked up from his newspaper and smiled.

Mrs. Buckworth said, "Um, Betti, we have plenty of eggs and toast if you're still hungry. You don't need to hurry, okay?"

"Okay." So I picked up another piece of red bread with my fork and started chewing it slowly around the edges.

The Buckworths would definitely want to send me home because I ate way too much and way too fast.

But then Lucy stabbed a piece of cooked bread with her fork and started eating it around the edges, just like me.

"Lucy . . ." said Mrs. Buckworth.

"I know." Lucy's cheeks puffed out as she grinned at me.

Then Mr. Buckworth picked up a piece of bread with his fork too. Lucy spit crumbs out of her mouth and started giggling like crazy with crumby teeth. I giggled a little too, because I couldn't help it.

Mrs. Buckworth sighed.

The Melon dog put his hairy head in my lap. He was everywhere. Lucy threw a piece of cooked bread toes to Rooney, who chomped it down in about one second and stared up at the sky to wait for more.

Ick.

I ate four pieces of red cooked bread and three gooey eggs, which must've made the ghosts very happy. I was like a pig eating sloppy slop and my stomach stuck out like a fat fruit.

I felt like I used to feel at the circus camp when I was up all night hearing things. Life in America was kind of like the circus. A new act every second. New sounds and smells and drooling animals and magic lotions and bouncing girls and bouncing bread toes. I never knew what would happen next.

MY EMPTY BOOK
(Second Day in America)

Ball Goons = Boom
Mikroo wave = Hot fast. No fire. No wood. No wave.
Ree-frigger-ater = For cold food.
Stove = For hot food.
Kichin = For eating my food.
Tele-veezion TV = Trapped prisoners.
Base Mint = Not for hiccups. Fat, jumping dog.
Spooogetti = Skinny broken-eyed snakes.
Yummy = To thank the snakes for letting me eat them.
Bed Rooom = For sleep. All mine but I don't want it.

Merrr-made = Half girl and half fish.

Nine Grade = Really old.

Peeelo = On bed for my head (but not comfortable like potato sack).

Pujamuzz = Fuzzy pink dress for sleep.

Overalzz = For poor farmers and me.

Swimming Soot = For swimming poo.

Little Tiger = ME.

Ick = Being good for ghosts. So I'll get more food.

Toes and Jellly = Cooked bread and red goo.

Break Fast = No break. Eat fast.

Empty Book = For showing Auntie Moo about the world of America.

Leftover Dogs and Plastic People

I WAS TRYING hard to hear the circus music.

Floating through the Buckworths' trees, or through their backyard, or through my open window or my skinny secret door. I was sure I'd still be able to hear it sometimes, all the way in America.

But I couldn't hear much of anything. Because after breakfast Mr. Buckworth was taking a bath and he was singing songs that made me stick my fingers in my ears.

Instead, while I was sitting in a corner, poking my toes into my fuzzy floor that was supposed to look like grass, I wrote new words in my Empty Book. I drew things, too: spaghetti snakes, and the television TV, and droolly dogs, and swimming mermaids with tails. I had to write and draw everything before I forgot. I touched my letter from Auntie Moo in the back of my book.

Finally Mr. Buckworth was done with his bath and his bad singing, and then it was Lucy's turn for a bath. She didn't sing but she did jump out of the bath and run into my yellow room with no clothes. She danced around and giggled like crazy until Mrs. Buckworth hollered for her to stop playing and to get back into the tub "immediately."

I closed my good eye so I could try and hear the left-over kids singing their long, sad songs around the fire circle. But before I could imagine much of anything, a little voice whispered in my ear. "Betti, are you sleeping?" A little finger touched my lips. Lucy had leaped back in—with clothes on, with soggy hair—and plopped down next to me.

I opened my good eye and closed my Empty Book.

"Do you want to play? I wonder if you will play with me?" Her head was tilted and she was smiling with no teeth. "Please?"

I was very busy with my book, but I was also very curious about Lucy's Melon games.

She had a whole bag filled with plastic dolls. She pulled them out one at a time, about ten of them, and lined them up next to my feet. All of her dolls were staring at me with perfect smiles.

"This is Jimmy Dale and Malibu Margie and Ramon

and Jessie Lynn, who's getting married. See? She has a wedding dress on.

"I got this doll . . . birth-day . . . I love her sooooo . . . much and I have . . . doll . . . house . . . really cute . . . Someday . . . I hope . . . car for dolls . . . maybe at Christmas . . . and maybe . . . Mom and Dad . . . they'll get you . . . house . . . too."

Gobbledygook. My head hurt from foreign words. It was easier when Auntie Moo spoke English to me because she only spoke the words I knew. Everybody here—except for Mrs. Buckworth—spoke too fast. And too loud. And spoke too many new important words.

Lucy's skinny dolls danced up and down in front of my face. Lucy's little hand made them march all the way up my arm and down again. "See, they're in a parade, Betti!" Lucy squealed. They bounced across Rooney's back, on top of his head, around my orange bag, and all over my stuffed circus bear.

Mrs. Buckworth poked her head in. "Betti, are you ready for your bath now?"

I scrunched my eyes and pretended that my ears were out of order.

"You really need to take one today, sweetie. This morning."

"No," I said. "Maybe at birthday. Maybe at Crissy-mess."

Mrs. Buckworth looked very confused. "At Christmas? But—"

"Mom," said Lucy, "we are busy now. She promises she'll take one later."

Mrs. Buckworth sighed. "Well . . . but—"

And fortunately that's when I heard the loud DONG-DONG noise from the front door. I heard: "Hi! Halllooo!"

GEORGE!

"Hi, Babo!"

I jumped up from the floor, leaped over to him, squeezed him around his belly, and nearly knocked him down. George and I bounced up and down as if we hadn't seen each other in a hundred years. Then George made woof-woof sounds at Rooney until Rooney licked his hand and drooled on the floor.

"Hi George!" said Lucy. "Will you play dolls with me?" She bounced her dolls all over George's feet until he giggled like crazy.

"Dulzz?" asked George. "O-kay." George always played anything.

In about one second, Lucy scampered out of my room. In another second she was back, holding a pink plastic house with tiny beds and chairs and tables inside. "This is where they live!" cheered Lucy, setting the fake house down on my floor with a thump.

George jumped off the bed and plopped down next to Lucy.

"You get to be Jessie Lynn," Lucy told him. "She's getting married."

George took the doll and looked at it up close. He had no clue what getting married meant, so I translated, and soon he was making Jessie Lynn run into every room in the dollhouse—the bedroom, the bathroom, the kitchen—as if he'd lived in a real house forever. He made Jessie Lynn say things like "Hi, hallooo. Hi, hallooo," and laughed as if it was the most fun he'd ever had in his whole life. Which just figured. Because I couldn't figure out what was so fun about playing with plastic people in a fake house. My games were definitely better.

So I took my circus doll and sat down on the floor too.

"Your doll doesn't really fit in, Betti," said Lucy. "She's a sock."

"She does not want to fit in house. She want to live in tent."

"*What?* What tent?" Lucy scrunched her eyes.

I pulled my blanket off the bed. George and I crawled under our circus tent. "Jessie Lynn," I told George's doll in our language, "it is time to feed the pigs."

George blabbered that he couldn't feed the pigs because he was getting married, and he already had his special occasion dress on, but I told him that was no excuse. The pigs needed their sloppy slop.

George shrugged. "O-kay." He loved my games.

"Now . . . you are Melon soldier," I told Lucy, pointing at the doll she was holding called Jimmy Dale. "You burn the house." I pointed at her pink dollhouse.

"You're bossy, Betti," said Lucy. "These are *my* dolls, not yours. Jimmy Dale goes to the beach, see? He gets tan."

"It is game. Do you want to play? Or not."

"Yeah, but . . . I don't want to burn my house."

I gathered all of her dolls under the tent except for Jimmy Dale. "Your Melon soldier has gun. But we are all mermaids."

George knew the English words "soldier" and "gun." In our real language he said, "Some soldiers are nice, Babo."

I sighed. "This is *my* game. This is *my* country."

"Your country is scary!" Lucy crossed her arms against her chest.

After I taught George what a mermaid was, he waved Jessie Lynn up and down as if she was diving in and out of the river. I made mine swim too. We flew our dolls all over the place, through the air and over the bed. Then George skipped off to the bathroom. When he ran back into my yellow room, Jessie Lynn and her wedding dress were dripping wet from swimming in the sink. George laughed like crazy.

"Now . . . all of circus people mermaids swim away. Saved."

"Banana," said George in English, meaning to say "fish." George made his hand into a big fish. "Soldier be eat." His hand ate Jimmy Dale in about one second and George threw the doll over his shoulder.

"And the ghosts in sky . . ." I said dramatically, "scare soldier. Forever."

George and I danced around my bedroom making "whoooo whoooo" ghost sounds. We jumped up on the bed and waved our arms around.

"NO!" shouted Lucy. "I HATE this game! I—"

George and I shook the blanket tent up and down and Lucy got caught under it. She flailed her legs and let out the loudest piercing screechy scream! It shook the house and made Rooney put his paw over his head.

Perfect.

If Lucy hated me—and my scary ghost games— she'd tell the Buckworths and they'd send me back to my country. Immediately.

She kept screaming and was wildly dashing out of my room, when . . .

She crashed into Mr. Buckworth. He stood in my open bedroom door chuckling. Mr. Buckworth probably thought we were having so much fun together, that I was teaching Lucy so many important things.

"I SCARE LUCY!" I cried.

Mr. Buckworth looked at Lucy and then at me. "Did you get scared, Luce?"

Lucy shrugged. "Nah. We were just playing. It was fun."

I sighed.

And Lucy forgot about horrible me, and my horrible games in about one second, because Mr. Buckworth had something hidden behind him. "Guess what, kids?" he said with a sly smile. "I have a little surprise!"

There were way too many surprises in America.

"What IS IT?" Lucy shouted, jumping up and down like crazy.

Then Mrs. Buckworth walked up behind Mr. Buckworth. She saw Mr. Buckworth's surprise first and gasped. "Larry, no! Not *another* one!"

It was a dog. Another one.

Mr. Buckworth told us that he had stopped at the store to pick up something for the special food that Mrs. Buckworth was going to make. "I couldn't just leave her there, could I? She looked so sad. All by herself. Just look at her!"

We all looked at her. I'd never seen such an ugly dog. She had big bald spots all over her chunky body, and crooked chewed ears, and one blue eye and one black eye. Mr. Buckworth put the dog on my bed, where she started to scratch like crazy until flakes of dry skin and patches of fur flew off.

"She's so CUTE!" squealed Lucy.

"CYOOOT!" cried George.

Which must've been the word for very, very ugly.

Mrs. Buckworth sighed. "Larry, we need another dog like we need a hole in the head."

"Just until we find her a good home—"

"And this one looks sick!"

"See? That's why I couldn't leave her outside the grocery store." Mr. Buckworth shook his head and flicked dog hair off his fancy suit. "She's just a sad little sick puppy."

"Larry," said Mrs. Buckworth with her hands on her hips, "that dog is at least fifteen years old. She is not a puppy. She is an elderly grandma!"

I didn't understand what an old dog had to do with a hole in the head, but just then the ugly dog jumped off my bed, squatted on my floor, and made a yellow spot. Ew.

"Let's call her Puddles!" cheered Lucy.

"Puttles!" repeated George.

Mrs. Buckworth sighed. She pointed out my bedroom door and told Mr. Buckworth to take *his* new dog outside so *his* new dog could learn to use the bathroom. Mr. Buckworth led the parade, with Rooney and Puddles and Lucy and George running after him.

Mrs. Buckworth went to the window in my room. She pulled back one side of the cloth covering the window and I pulled back the other. Mr. Buckworth was trying to get Puddles to sit, and finally Puddles sat and peed on Mrs. Buckworth's purple flowers. George was running around the backyard hollering WOOF WOOF. Lucy was trying to get Rooney to jump over an empty swinging seat, but Rooney wanted to itch his ear with his paw. Mrs. Buckworth looked at me and sighed.

She explained that Mr. Buckworth had a little problem with saving animals. He was the Vice President of a bank, but he would really prefer being the Vice President of a home for lost dogs.

That's when I thought: This is bad. Very, very bad. If the Buckworths saved an ugly elderly lost dog, and didn't send her back to the grocery store, I was never going to get sent home.

Sloppy Slop

WE PLAYED OUTSIDE all day.

Mr. and Mrs. Buckworth pushed George and Lucy and me in the swinging seats, and I felt like I was going to shoot straight over their house and into the sky. George squealed like a flying baby monkey.

There was also this game we played called something like "hide-and-squeak." I squatted and hid in the bushes. When Lucy found me, I danced around like a ghost and squeaked and squeaked, but she wasn't even a bit scared this time. She just giggled.

I didn't know if it was a good thing or a bad thing to be "it," but when Mr. Buckworth was it, and he found me, he let out a roar that almost made me jump out of my flip-flops. I screamed like crazy and ran around the Buckworths' yard.

I forgot all about being bad. I wanted to swing on the seats. I wanted to play hide-and-squeak.

We started to play this Melon game called "bad mitten" where Mr. Buckworth put up a net, and told us we had to hit a birdy. George's bottom lip stuck out and he said he didn't want to hit a birdy, when suddenly Lucy started sniffing with her nose in the air. Then George and Mr. Buckworth and I sniffed too. It was a very funny smell. Coming from the kitchen.

"Ew," said Lucy. "Pew. PU."

Lucy plugged her nose, so George plugged his nose too. "Pee You," said George, which must've been the Melon words for rotten vegetables that had been trampled by pigs during a drought. That's when Mrs. Buckworth called us inside for a special dinner.

"My name Mister Buckworth," said Mrs. Buckworth.

George and I raised our eyebrows at each other. He covered his mouth with his hand.

"Me name . . . is Larry," tried Mr. Buckworth. "Me love . . . dog."

Mrs. Buckworth snorted.

Then George's mommy spoke: "My baby's name . . . George. He . . . beautiful."

George puffed out his chest and beamed while I scrunched my eyes at him. He was way too old to be a baby. And *beautiful*?

"I am . . . a . . . cockroach?" said Mrs. Buckworth, flipping through the pages of the big book. George tilted his head and I made a little groan. We had no idea what Mrs. Buckworth was trying to say.

Mr. Buckworth thought really hard and itched the top of his head. "I have . . . bug hairy hair," he spit out. I bit my tongue and George laughed like crazy because he couldn't help it.

George's mommy and the Buckworths were trying to learn some words in our language.

"At least they're trying, Babo," said George quietly.

At least they were trying. Even if they sounded like three-year-olds from our country. With bad brains.

Unfortunately, Mrs. Buckworth was also trying to make food from our country. She found a recipe in the big book on the living room table, which was also where she found the language lessons.

We stared at the pretty bowl that Mrs. Buckworth put on the table. What was inside the bowl wasn't pretty at all. Brown mush. Enough for about twenty leftover kids.

"Vomit," said Lucy.

"Vahmitt," repeated George.

Which must've been the word for pig sloppy slop in a bowl.

We all put a glob of it on our plates.

"You guys actually eat this stuff every day?" Lucy asked George and me, scrunching up her whole face.

"Don't you even mix it with sugar? Or jelly? Or any-thing?"

George and I shrugged and looked down at our bowls as Mr. Buckworth raised his glass and announced, "This is a toast to Betti and George! To your new lives in America!"

I scanned the table for cooked bread toes, but didn't see a single piece. There was only mush.

"A toast to Betti and George!" cheered Mrs. Buckworth and George's mommy. "We're so happy you're here!"

"Me too," said Lucy. "'Cause Betti likes to play with me."

I sighed.

Rooney licked George's hand under the table and Puddles stood up and howled. Everyone clinked glasses together, so I clinked mine too.

George's mommy was the first to pick up her spoon. She tried a bite. "Mmmm, very tasty." She puckered her lips together and her eyes grew huge.

Then Mr. Buckworth tried it. "Mmmm." His eyes darted under the table in search of a dog. "Good work, honey! Mmm-hmm."

I tried a bite. George and Lucy did too.

We all put our spoons down and drank some milk.

Lucy glared at me like the sloppy slop was my fault. "Ick, Betti," she said. "This is totally gross."

"Ick." I thanked the ghosts for my sloppy slop, even though it was totally "gross." Which must've been the word for strange foods that made people's fingernails turn orange.

Mrs. Buckworth finally tasted a spoonful and said, "Hmmm. Well . . . it is very interesting, isn't it?" The rest of us nodded, while Mrs. Buckworth smiled at me hopefully. Usually I ate everything on my banana leaf plate. Every single bite.

Sister Baroo told us that we should always eat everything—never waste—because someday we might be starving. We had to store up, just like camels had to store water so they wouldn't die in the desert. But with Mrs. Buckworth's special dish I really didn't want to be a camel.

George and I looked at each other as my stomach growled at me. Even though George is weird he's still the one who understands everything. Neither of us had the guts to tell Mrs. Buckworth that we'd never seen that mush before in our whole lives. No one was crazy enough to eat that stuff in our country.

"BETTI? IT'S TIME for your bath now, sweetie."

George and his mommy had just left after the gross vomit dinner. And Lucy and I had just finished our important job of carrying dishes from the table to Mrs. Buckworth, who was washing them.

I dropped three dirty napkins and a fork on the floor. "I take my bath with pigs."

Mrs. Buckworth laughed. "We don't have pigs here in the house, Betti, but—"

"I bath in my river."

Mrs. Buckworth's smile faded, just a little. "We have a bathtub here, Betti. You're going to take a bath in the bathtub."

I picked at a hole in my circus dress. "I bath in my dress."

"I'll wash your dress afterward. I'll get it really clean, okay?"

"I wash my dress." I knocked my flip-flops together. "On rocks."

Mr. Buckworth stood up from the eating table. "Come on, little tiger." He held my hand and started to lead me to the bathroom.

"It's really not so bad, Betti." Mrs. Buckworth sounded worried, so it was probably very, very bad.

Mrs. Buckworth didn't understand anything.

And neither did Mr. Buckworth. Before I knew it, he picked me up in his big hairy bear arms, and chuckled as he bounced me up and down and held me over his shoulder like a sack of potatoes.

Mrs. Buckworth followed and so did Lucy, who was skipping behind us as if this was the most interesting thing that had ever happened at the Buckworths' house.

I grabbed on to the bathroom door as tightly as I could but my fingers slipped.

And that's when I starting kicking, just like a little tiger. "I—DO NOT—WANT—BATH!" I accidentally pulled out a few pieces of Mr. Buckworth's copper coin hair. I bugged out my good eye and made the biggest meanest growl I could straight at Lucy.

Lucy stopped in her tracks and her giggling stopped immediately. "Mom," she whimpered in a tiny voice.

As Mr. Buckworth set me down and left the bathroom, Mrs. Buckworth put her arm around me and rubbed my back. "I'm so sorry if you don't like this at first, Betti, but you really do need to take a bath."

At the circus camp no one cared that I smelled because everyone smelled and that's the way things were. I used to bathe in the river once a week, of course, just like the pigs. But Mrs. Buckworth said that *here* little girls bathe every single day because it is summer, and summer is hot, and it is not good to smell.

"I LIKE to DIRTY!" I cried. "I LIKE to SMELL!"

In less than about one second Mrs. Buckworth had pulled my dress over my head and removed my flip-flops and my ratty underwear, and had lowered me into the horrible water trough bathtub. "In you go, my dear."

None of them understood that I didn't want to be scrubbed until I was blue and raw and wrinkled like a baby elephant. And I definitely couldn't take off my circus dress. If my circus dress got stolen I'd have nothing left. If it was washed, the circus camp would be washed away. That's when I reached over the edge and whisked my circus dress off the floor. I held it over my head and squeezed it and wouldn't let go.

"Betti, your dress—"

"It is me. It is mine!"

When Mrs. Buckworth kneeled down and put some goop on my head and scrunched it around making lots of bubbles, I splashed and splashed.

My dress fell out of my hand and into the water. It floated. So I ducked my whole head under the water, and sat on my dress, and that made everyone quiet.

I was a mermaid. Some water went into my open mouth and it didn't taste anything like the piggy river. It was good water, clean, so I swallowed more, making bubbles like a blowfish.

From underwater I heard Lucy say, "See? It's not that bad, Betti."

It was bad. My dress was clean just like the water, just like me.

This was war.

Gobbledygook and a Dress

"SOMETIMES . . . MAY HAVE to do things . . . don't want to do . . . Not trying to be mean, Betti . . . You can believe . . . that. Just part of . . . being a little girl . . . here."

Mrs. Buckworth had tried to dry me off with a fuzzy towel before I ran from the bathroom clutching my dress. I'd slammed the door to my yellow room. I'd thrown on my wet circus dress and jumped into my bed.

"Don't worry . . . work it out together. Day by day . . . learn about each other, okay? Never . . . never do anything . . . to hurt . . . you . . ."

Gobbledygook.

The Buckworths looked upset as they stood over my bed. Mrs. Buckworth put her hand on my cheek and brushed wet hair out of my eyes. Mr. Buckworth sighed.

"We love you, sweetie."

"We really do."

Maybe the Buckworths' brains were out of order. They didn't seem to understand that I was bad. Very, very bad. I talked about ghosts and I didn't like to use a fork. I hated baths and I told Lucy about guns and soldiers and falling-out hair.

"No," I said. "Do not love . . ." I pulled the covers over my head and said in a scratchy muffled tiger voice, "Me."

Finally they turned out the light and left. I was quiet in my bed, in the dark. I waited until the whole Buckworth house was very quiet. And that's when I threw off those stupid covers and stood up shivering in my wet dress. I went to the secret door and opened it so I could stare at all of my new Melon clothes.

Trying on my new clothes for a second couldn't hurt anything.

I took off my circus dress and very carefully put on a blue special occasion dress. Then I put on my red buckle special occasion shoes. I pointed my toes gracefully and walked back and forth on an invisible line with my fingers curled up. Just perfectly, just like a circus star. Even though I wanted to show Mrs. Buckworth how I looked in my new dress—she'd probably tell me again how pretty I was, the most beautiful girl in the world—I was still mad. Very, very mad.

I twirled and twirled on the fuzzy fake grass, and twirled some more. I was just going to try on another brand-new dress, when I discovered . . . the glass on the inside of the door. My face stared back at me. I was pretty sure it was me. I used to see my face in the river, but the water was murky and so was my face. But here? Way too clear.

I put my nose right up against the glass. It was definitely a girl with a normal eye and a fish eye. Me.

Both of my eyes were gray like smoke. My good eye blinked, but my bad eye was looking somewhere else. At something *very* important. My bad eye had probably seen all sorts of things before it got hurt. It made me look like a foreign monster, a freaky mermaid that crawled out of the sea. Everyone in my country looked sort of freaky, in one way or another, but in America nobody had an eye like mine.

Lucy was right. My circus doll would never fit in. And I would never fit in either, which was fine by me. I couldn't be a Melon because I didn't want to be a traitor.

Someday soon the leftover kids would be very happy with our new clothes. They'd take turns wearing the birthday party dress and fight over the pajamas. They'd skip through prickly vines in the red buckle shoes and giggle in the swimming suit as they rode on the pigs.

But for now I was still here and they were still there. They didn't have a whole bunch of clothes hanging like empty people. They didn't have a room as big as the lion cage. They didn't have spaghetti snakes and bread toes. They were hungry like I used to be hungry.

I took off that stupid blue dress and put my wet circus dress back on. I opened my jar of circus camp dirt and sprinkled a little all over my dress so it'd stick like mud. I slipped my flip-flops back on, put my potato sack under my arm, stuffed my circus bear and my circus doll and all of Lucy's smiling dolls in my orange bag and flung it over my shoulder.

I was very good at walking so softly that no one could ever hear me. I used to walk like this—and sometimes I ran—all the way to the village to find out what was happening. I had to tell Auntie Moo and the leftover kids if our village was on fire. I had to go door to door in the village and warn people. I was a messenger. I was used to the dark and I never made a peep.

So the Buckworths definitely didn't hear a peep as I snuck outside followed by that hairy old Rooney and ugly Puddles. I lay down next to the empty seat swings under the tree. My hair was wet and it smelled funny, but not as bad as Rooney's breath, which kept blowing in my face. I lined up all the dolls next to Rooney and Puddles on the grass.

The sky was dark blue and black. I shivered again in my soggy dress, and then I sneezed.

I thought about things for a long time, and wondered if time at the circus camp was the same as time in America. I hoped that a leftover kid was watching the sky to see if anything was coming.

Rooney was staring at me. Puddles was scratching herself. I knew they were curious about what happened to my real mom and dad—all the circus people—and why I had to be here.

"The village people say that the circus camp is haunted," I told the dogs and the dolls in my real language. *"Some people say that the circus people got taken to a prison camp for freaks. Other people think they were sent off on a boat and out to sea so no one except for fish and sharks would have to look at them again. Some people say they were taken across the border and kept in cages where audiences laughed at them instead of clapping. Old Lady Suri from the bean stand says that they just disappeared to a better place where ghosts live. In the trees and in the sky."*

Puddles put her patchy fur paw on top of my arm.

"But I'm the only smart one who knows that they escaped. I know that they're still singing. They're still saying, 'Babo and the rest of us may look funny, we may not look alike, but we're a family and you can never hurt us.'"

Quiet tears ran from my good eye onto my wet dress.

That's when Rooney licked my face with his slimy tongue. It wasn't quite so nice as having the leftover kids smooshed against me, but the dogs were warm. And I think the dogs, and my circus bear and circus doll, and all of Lucy's plastic smiling dolls, understood my story better than Melon people.

I sneezed again and rubbed my arms, which had bumps from the cold.

America is a cold, cold place.

And this was only my second day.

I trudged back into the Buckworths' house, followed by Rooney and Puddles. We went back to the yellow room. I put my fuzzy warm pajama dress back on, because wearing my pajama dress once in a while couldn't hurt anything. Then I climbed back into my bed because I didn't have anywhere else to go. My real home was way too far away.

Trapped

"WE'VE GOT TO get out of here."

George's mouth was puffed out from cookies. He grabbed another one. "Why, Babo?"

It was my third day in America, the next afternoon. Mr. Buckworth was being a Vice President somewhere and Lucy got to go somewhere called "Day Camp."

"Can Betti go too, Mom?" Lucy asked at the eating table in the morning. "Pleasssssse?"

I wondered if Day Camp was like the circus camp, at least a little. I definitely wanted to go. But Mrs. Buckworth said that I couldn't go to Day Camp because I had something else to do.

So George was stuck with me at the Buckworths' house. He had on brand-new clothes, of course. His hair was slicked back and parted on the side. We were sitting right next to each other on the Buckworths' fluffy sofa swinging our legs back and forth.

"Haven't you noticed? People in this country are . . . crazy!" I bugged out my good eye, but George just fidgeted in his new striped play shirt. "And it's *very* dangerous here, George. And cold."

We both ate another cookie. We were supposed to be waiting to talk to some Melon lady, just like we always waited for Melons at the circus camp.

"You're going to meet a very nice woman from the adoption agency, kids," Mrs. Buckworth had told us as she set a plate of little round things on the living room table and kneeled down in front of us. "It'll be nice for you to talk to her. You can ask her lots of questions, okay? She understands what it's like to be in a new country. What it's like to be adopted."

George didn't really care who the nice lady was, and couldn't understand Mrs. Buckworth anyway.

I rolled my eyes and translated to George: "This lady is coming to tell us all the reasons we should be Melons." George tilted his head and nodded. "She's going to tell us that we better like it here or we'll be in big trouble."

George was more interested in the plate that Mrs. Buckworth had set on the table. "These are called 'cookies,' kids," she said.

"Koookies?" I asked suspiciously.

"Koookies," repeated George.

"I think you'll like them." Mrs. Buckworth smiled. Then she went back to the kitchen, where she was drinking coffee with George's mommy.

We both looked at our cookies up close. They were two black circles with white in the center. Perfect animal manure patties. We both bit in at the same time. Hmmmm. We chewed some more. Then we each stuffed a whole cookie in our mouths.

"Yummy," I said, to thank the animals for letting us eat their manure patties.

"Yummy," repeated George.

He reached out and grabbed two more cookies and I grabbed three.

As we were crunching away, I heard Mrs. Buckworth talking to George's mommy. I couldn't hear much, but I did hear Mrs. Buckworth saying something about "bath" and "her dress" and "on the first morning we found her outside."

"Outside?" asked George's mommy, as if this was the strangest thing that had ever happened in America.

"I just don't think she likes it here. She seems so unhappy."

"George," I said, grabbing him by the hand and pulling him off the sofa. His cookie fell out of his mouth onto the fuzzy floor. He looked back at it. "I have to show you something."

I walked him straight to the television TV and plunked him down in front of it.

"It is called TV, Babo," said George. "I like TV."

"I know what it's called." I sighed and started pacing back and forth. "George, you're still a little kid, and you don't understand English. But it's just like I told you before. See, George, these people in the TV are saying, 'Help! Help me!'"

George put his nose up to the television. "They are?" He knocked on it. "Halllooooo. Halloooooo." There was a Melon boy on the TV with his hair parted just like George's.

"They can't hear you. They're trapped. The Melons put them in there."

George looked up at me. He was very worried. "What did they do that was so bad?"

"I'm not sure exactly. Maybe they said they weren't afraid, just like the circus people. So the soldiers took them and put them in TV jail. Prisoners of War in America. Like our country, but different."

"But Auntie Moo said there was no war in Amer—"

"You're not listening. This is very important."

George leaned back on his ankles and rocked back and forth. He pressed his hand gently against the TV and tried to follow a TV person with his finger. "I'd help them if I knew how to get them out. I'd let them go free, Babo."

"Me too."

We both scooted behind the TV to see if there was a secret door that we could open. But there was no door and no people. Just black plastic. I poked my finger through a hole in the back, and George stuck his eye into another hole. "I can't see anybody, Babo."

"No." I shook my head. "Those poor, poor prisoners."

"Scary," said George.

"Very scary."

We looked at each other and shrugged.

"But Babo," said George, "they look sort of happy in jail." The people were singing and dancing, smiling the biggest, whitest smiles I'd ever seen. "They don't look sad."

I sighed. "That doesn't mean much at all."

Then we heard the DONG DONG noise at the front door. We heard Mrs. Buckworth and George's mommy say "hello hello" and we heard a stranger's voice.

"The nice lady!" cried George. "She must be here."

I jumped up and pulled George with me. "Come on. Hurry."

"But—"

I picked up the whole plate of cookies and we ran into my yellow room. I went immediately to the secret skinny door in my bedroom. First I took out my orange bag and opened it and threw half the plate of cookies inside. Then I made George sit down next to me so we could stare straight into the mirror glass.

"Now look, George. Look at you."

George looked at himself. He tilted his head one way, and then the other.

"Scary."

"I know. You're very scary. See? The Melons are trying to make you an American already."

"I like Amair-ee—ka, Babo," said George.

"That's not the point!"

George kept staring into the mirror. He slowly traced his finger along the glass. "Look, Babo! It's like I have two fingers that match! I have two arms and two hands. They're exactly the same."

I rolled my good eye. "George, you do not have two arms. It's a trick, see?"

George wasn't listening because he was too busy wiggling his ears and looking at them in the mirror. He giggled. He flapped his arm like a bird, and smiled a big smile even though his teeth were dirty from cookies. George was fascinated with himself, as if he was the most beautiful boy in the whole world.

"Kids!" Mrs. Buckworth called from the other room.

I whispered, "Don't you remember what I told you? Melons will try to change you from the inside out. Your brain will get messy. And you're really close to becoming a Melon, George. You've already changed."

George was quiet. He looked at me very seriously. "I haven't changed, Babo. I'm still just me. George."

"No. You're being tricked like the prisoners in the TV are being tricked. You have to be careful. You have to listen carefully to the stories your mommy tells you. Don't believe a single word."

"My mommy?"

"Especially your mommy."

George immediately stood up from the floor. "She's not a Melon, Babo!"

George never disagreed with me. This was bad. Very, very bad.

I thought about things. "Yeah, but that's why it's tricky, George. See, your mommy already loves you. And if she loves you too much she'll never send you back. That is exactly why you have to be a *horrible* boy. You have to be *so* horrible that—"

"Kids! She's here!" cried George's mommy. "George! Betti!"

My important lesson was over in one second because George ran out of my room as if some royal princess had arrived.

And me? I crawled under my bed with my blanket and covered my head.

I heard George giggling. Which just figured.

"Betti? Would you like to come on out?" It was Mrs. Buckworth.

"She . . . donkey bed," said George.

"*Under* bed," I mumbled to myself. "Not donkey."

George was going to get himself thrown into the zoo with his lousy English.

Soon I thought they forgot all about me. But I wasn't so lucky. There was about a whole ten minutes of George giggling and trying to speak English. Everybody always loves George.

Then the Melon adoption lady came into my room. "Betti, are you in here? Won't you come out and talk to me? Even for a minute?"

I lowered the blanket and peeked out. All I saw were her shoes. Special occasion shoes. Yellow. And tall.

"Well, that's okay. I'll talk to you from here, if you don't mind. I'm Lenore. I've been helping kids who've been adopted for twenty years. A long time, Betti. So I know a little about what you're going through."

The adoption lady may have been some sort of expert on adopted leftover kids, but she wasn't an expert on me.

I took the blanket off my head so the adoption lady could hear my Big Mouth. "Are you from my country?" I asked her in my language.

There was a pause. "Uh, unfortunately I only speak English. In fact, I'm going to start teaching you and George some English. Would that be okay with you?"

"No."

"Why is that? I know you speak pretty well already, Betti, but it might help to learn more, don't you think? For when you start school?"

"Auntie Moo is my teacher."

"Auntie Moo, of course. Well, but, Auntie Moo's still back in your country, Betti."

"I know!" I practically growled.

"So you'll need school here too."

"Auntie Moo is my school!"

I heard the adoption lady sigh. "Think about it, okay? Will you think about it? Please?"

I thought about it already. There was silence.

"And . . . I also want to talk to you about how things are going so far. I wonder how you like America?" Lenore really liked to talk.

"America . . . no baths in river," I blurted out. "No pigs, no monkeys. No market like my market. No circus music, no story like my story, no lion cage, no sleep at night with kids, no good games like my games, no Old Lady Suri. She tell me I will not come back. Lost like ghost. But I am not a ghost."

"Of course you're not a ghost, Betti, but—"

"But it is *okay*." I scooted out on my back from under my bed, so I was staring straight up at Lenore. "Because my mama and dad will come. To take me home. Probably tomorrow. They fly on airplane. In sky."

Lenore shuffled her feet. She looked down at me, and looked away, and looked down at me again. Her lips twitched. Her eyes were sad slivers. "Betti, you know . . . about your mother and father . . . what happened . . . won't be coming, dear . . . I know . . . that's hard to hear . . ."

Gobbledygook. The adoption lady was just a voice. And shoes.

". . . the Buckworths . . . nice family . . . they love . . . have to . . . give them a chance. Who knows? Maybe you'll even like it here."

And that's exactly when I scrunched back under my bed and pulled the covers back over my head. All except for my good eye, peeking out, that had to watch everything. I let out a snort like a cow.

The shoes finally left my room.

"She'll adapt," I heard the voice say to Mrs. Buckworth. "Don't worry . . . starts school . . . learns more English . . . makes some friends . . . gets used to things . . . She will."

I had no idea what the word "adapt" meant. But it was close enough to the word "adopt." I would not stay adopted, and I had to try very hard not to adapt.

Santy Claws and the Fairy with Teeth

IT FELT LIKE a whole bunch of hours went by, but maybe it was just a few minutes. It was hard to say.

"Betti?" said a very soft voice.

It wasn't the adoption Melon lady's voice; it was Mrs. Buckworth's.

I wasn't even going to come out for Mrs. Buckworth. I wanted to stay under my bed forever. But I peeked out and saw Mrs. Buckworth lying down on the floor too. She was looking under my bed. At me.

"I did not want to talk. To nice lady." I covered my eyes again.

"That's all right. Maybe some other time."

I snorted.

"Betti, do you mind if I tell you a story?"

"Is it a good story?" My voice was all muffled.

Mrs. Buckworth laughed. "I don't know about that. Some parts are good, some bad. Not as good as your stories, I'm sure."

I took the blanket off my head anyway because I was curious about Mrs. Buckworth's Big Mouth story.

She took a big breath and began: "So . . . there was a little girl, a long, long time ago, who lost her parents."

My good eye got big. "She lost them? Where did they go?"

"The girl wasn't sure. One day they just disappeared."

"Like ghosts?" I stared at Mrs. Buckworth sideways. I picked at the fuzzy fake grass on my floor.

"Well, yeah. I guess you could say that."

"Maybe a bomb?" I added quickly. "Or they washed away in river?"

"The girl didn't want to think about those things." Mrs. Buckworth sighed and stared off for a second, thinking. "She couldn't think bad thoughts."

I bumped my head on my bed, and inched my way out from under it. "So she look for them. All over the whole world?"

"Well, she was very little. Much younger than you. She thought her mom and dad wouldn't be gone for long. She thought they'd be coming home any day."

"And they did!" I practically shouted.

Mrs. Buckworth shook her head sadly. "No . . . instead she got shipped off to all sorts of other places. Other homes."

"On a ship?" I crossed my legs and sat in front of Mrs. Buckworth. I liked this story.

"Well, not really on a ship." Mrs. Buckworth sat up and crossed her legs too. "First . . . she was sent to some relatives' houses. She'd never even met them before. Three different houses. Total strangers. They weren't mean strangers; they just didn't really want a little girl. Some of the relatives were old. She made them tired. Some of them were too busy. 'We're sorry,' they said. So she got sent off *again.* In the next home, with foster parents, they didn't really want her either. Or the home after that. They had too many kids."

"Was the little girl really bad?"

"Oh, she got into all sorts of trouble. She made other kids get into trouble too!" Mrs. Buckworth laughed a little, so I did too. She nodded to herself. "It made some sense that they didn't really want her. But, the thing is, she wasn't a bad girl."

"She was not bad?"

"No. She was just a sad girl. The saddest girl you could ever imagine. The saddest girl in the whole world."

My good eye got cloudy to think about such a sad, sad girl.

Mrs. Buckworth's eyes got cloudy too. "The only thing that made her happy was thinking about when her real mom and dad would come to save her. Then she'd be happy again; she was sure of it. So she kept waiting and waiting. But they didn't come for her. Soon she couldn't even remember their voices or what they looked like. She started to think that her dad was a very important person: Santa Claus!"

"Santy Claws?"

Mrs. Buckworth spread her arms out really wide. "A *big* old man with a beard and a kind smile. The nicest man in the world. But . . . he was so busy that he could only come once a year. She never got to see him exactly, but he brought her presents."

"Like an Empty Book?"

Mrs. Buckworth shook her head sadly. "No, I wish she would've had an Empty Book. She also began to imagine that her mom was the Tooth Fairy. So important that she could only come and visit when the girl had a tooth fall out. The girl started to look forward to losing her teeth! Once she even tried to pull some out herself."

"Ew." I scrunched my face.

"Every night she would lie in her bed and dream. And wait."

"Sweet dreams or bad dreams?" I was already dreaming about the pictures I'd draw about Mrs. Buckworth's story in my Empty Book: Santy Claws, the Ghost Fairy of Teeth, the sad little girl.

"Both, I guess. She would dream that Santa Claus and the Tooth Fairy would take her home somewhere far away." Mrs. Buckworth tilted her head and looked closely at me, straight into my good eye and my bad eye. "That was her wish. That was the present she wanted."

"Did Santy Claws and Tooth Lady bring her the present?"

"No. They never did. The girl thought it was her fault. She felt so alone. And trapped too. Because she was so little and didn't know where to go."

"So . . ." I scooted forward and put my elbows on Mrs. Buckworth's feet. "What did she do?"

"The girl decided to run away." Mrs. Buckworth got very dramatic. "She wanted to find her mom and dad all by herself."

My good eye bugged out. Mrs. Buckworth's story was very interesting. It was a good one. "But . . . how?"

"Easy. Marched right out the door when no one was looking." She nodded toward my bedroom door to make her point.

"But . . . where did she go?"

"Well, she made it to the corner, just down the street. She was already cold and hungry. She didn't have any food or money. She missed having a home where it was warm. The foster parents could be warm too, sometimes. It definitely wasn't perfect, but she realized that she had to let people help her, a little at least."

"But her mama and dad . . . they did come. Yes? They help her."

"No, Betti. They couldn't come because they had died when she was so little."

"They died? In the war?"

"No, not a war. It was just a bad accident. But she didn't understand that until much later. Her mom and dad couldn't come, but it wasn't her fault. Some people had told her the truth all along, but she still had to believe they were coming back."

"Then what happened to little girl?"

"Well, she grew up, like little girls do."

"She did never get adopted?"

"No." Mrs. Buckworth shrugged. "Never adopted. But soon she was old enough to go out into the world by herself."

"Alone?"

"Yes, but the girl was strong. And brave. She tried to remember good things. One thing she remembered was that her mom's name had been Betti."

"Betti? That's *your* mama's name."

Mrs. Buckworth nodded slowly. She looked down at her lap.

"It is a true story?"

"Yup. The true story about me. I always wanted a family." Mrs. Buckworth touched my cheek. "I feel so lucky to have one now, Betti," she said quietly. "I got my wish."

I didn't have any Big Mouth words in any language.

Mrs. Buckworth stood up and put her hand gently on my head, and then she left my yellow room.

I felt sad for Mrs. Buckworth, the saddest little girl in the world. Her parents were killed and she thought that her dad was Santy Claws, some hairy man with claws, and her mom was a Fairy Ghost who made kids pull out their teeth. Nobody loved her, so she ran away because she was so alone and lonely. If Mrs. Buckworth would've run to the circus camp she could've been a leftover kid too. Then she would've been loved, really loved. I would've watched over her every day and made sure she was okay.

But Mrs. Buckworth had been a little girl, younger than me. I was already brave, like a little tiger. I was already old enough to go out into the world by myself. I didn't need any help.

Mrs. Buckworth may not have been a bad girl, but I was. Horrible, even. But I'd have to be worse, much, much worse. And if the Buckworths *still* couldn't realize how bad I was, if they *still* loved me, then . . .

I'd have to run away.

MY EMPTY BOOK
(Day Three in America)

Pew Pee You = Bad smell. Like rotten vegetables.
   Must plug nose.

Hole in head = Mr. Buckworth has a hole in his head?
   Mrs. Buckworth mad.

Cyooot = Very ugly.

Puttles = Peeing on the floor. Ugly dog.

Vomitt = Pig sloppy slop in a bowl.

Gross = Orange fingernails from strange food.

Day Camp = Like Circus Camp?

Koooky = Sweet animal manure patty.

Santy Claws = Hairy Man with claws. Brings present.

Fairy Ghost of Teeth = Makes children pull their
   teeth out.

Adapt = Adopt = Become a Melon

Crazy America

IN MY COUNTRY danger could strike at any second. It was life or death. You had to be on guard at all times. You had to listen for any little noise, any movement, any strange smell. You had to lie low and wait for the right time to escape.

That's what I had to do in America.

I had to wait for the right time to run away. So I definitely had to stay another day. Or two. Or just a few.

And in just a few more days I realized that Melons were even crazier than I thought.

Especially the Buckworths.

Mrs. Buckworth taught me how to scrub my teeth with a teeth brush, and used the same nasty goo paste that was always donated to the Mission. I didn't tell Mrs. Buckworth that we used that stuff to fill the holes in our flip-flops. After I brushed my teeth, I spit my goo paste at Lucy before I learned that I was supposed to spit in the sink. Lucy thought it was funny, and spit her goo at me, but I don't think Mrs. Buckworth thought that was a bit funny.

I took baths too, because the water was very warm and clean. And so far I hadn't turned raw and wrinkled and blue. A few baths couldn't hurt anything. On my fourth day in America I even sang a long, sad song in the bathtub about the war in my country and how it never stopped.

After my bath, Mrs. Buckworth tried to comb out my hair nice and straight in front of the bathroom mirror. "Would you like ponytails, Betti? Like Lucy?" asked Mrs. Buckworth. Lucy's hair stuck out both sides of her head like red horns. Pony tails. But my hair is very unique, that's what Auntie Moo says. Circus hair. So I said no to Mrs. Buckworth because I didn't want to look like a pony or a tail or a Melon.

On my fifth day in America, Mr. Buckworth took George and me shopping. He was supposed to be the Vice President somewhere, but Mr. Buckworth said that he would much rather be riding around with George and me than sitting behind a "big old boring desk, at a boring bank, with boring bank people."

Instead, Mr. Buckworth liked to point at things as we were driving around in the wagon.

"Do you see *that*, kids? That's called a bicycle. We're going to get you one soon, Betti, okay? And look, there's a house in the tree! It's called a 'tree house.' Kids climb into it, see? For fun."

George and I nodded. A bicycle. A tree house.

Mr. Buckworth was driving very slowly, like Big Uncle in his taxi, so lots of cars zoomed by us and honked. He waved out his window at a woman rolling a baby on wheels. After we drove by, Mr. Buckworth said, "That baby looks sort of like a monkey, wouldn't you say, kids?"

He also pointed out a skateboard and a stop sign and a motorcycle driven by a woman in a striped hard hat. A garden and a park and some ducks quacking around a pond.

"Quack quack," said George.

A mailman. A mailbox. A dog peeing on a mailbox. George and I giggled.

"Look there, kids." Mr. Buckworth pointed. "That's called a porch."

I looked up at the tilted porch in front of the tilted house.

I saw the very same girl who'd been reading a book on the porch when I first came to America. The girl who was maybe a circus girl, even if she was a Melon. This time the girl was building a tower in a tall jungle of grass that came up to her waist. It was a tower made out of pots and pans and rusty cans and who knows what else. She looked up at me and I waved, because I didn't know what else to do. She waved back and her hand stayed there, just like that. Then her tower crashed down and got buried in grass.

That's when something rang in Mr. Buckworth's pocket that nearly made me jump out of my circus dress. "Hello?" said Mr. Buckworth, talking into the little magic thing.

"Hi. Halloo," answered George.

Actually, Mr. Buckworth was talking to himself. He asked himself questions and then he waited and answered himself.

George and I looked at each other and shrugged. Crazy.

"Sorry, kids," said Mr. Buckworth. "That was just boring business."

Americans seemed very, very busy doing busy-ness, zooming around, talking to themselves, even though I wasn't sure exactly what anyone was doing. I poked the side of Mr. Buckworth's seat so he'd stop itching his head and talking to himself.

As Mr. Buckworth was parking the wagon, I asked if this was his village market. He said yes. Sort of.

Once a week Auntie Moo would walk down to the market, and all the leftover kids would follow behind like ducks. It was our favorite day of the whole week.

People came from everywhere to sell vegetables and meats and sweets. Once Auntie Moo had her bag of oats stolen at the market from a man who poked her in the back.

And me? Usually I listened to Old Lady Suri tell long stories about the Melons and America at her bean stand.

"Little funny one," she'd say to me in her crackly old voice as she chewed on a big hunk of tobacco, "our people leave this country and never come back. They just disappear." Old Lady Suri shook her head as she shook her beans. Her hundred-year-old hands plucked out the dirt and crawly bugs. "It makes our ghosts very upset, you see. That is why our country stays haunted with bad luck."

"Are you guys hungry?" asked Mr. Buckworth. George and I nodded, but we were always hungry, so that didn't mean much. Mr. Buckworth took us to a special part of the market where they gave food to people who sat in plastic orange chairs at shiny blue tables.

"Is food free?" I asked.

"Well, yes," replied Mr. Buckworth. "*You* don't have to pay for it, Betti. You don't have to worry about that, okay?"

I was worried, but not for long, because soon food was on the plastic table in front of George and me. We each had a cardboard box with pictures of funny monsters. French fry, Coca-Cola, hot dog, Mr. Buckworth told us as I gobbled up the french fry and drank the free Coca-Cola.

I stared at my hot dog. It was probably a tail. Rooney and Puddles were okay. For Melon dogs. They came outside with me at night and listened very carefully to my stories. I didn't think it was very nice to eat a cooked dog, but George didn't care. He stuffed mine in his mouth in about one second.

When Mr. Buckworth went to get more free Coca-Cola, a Melon woman walked by. She looked at me, and then at my bad eye. She tried to look away, but she had to look at my bad eye again—a sad second look—as if I'd just exploded in a puff of smoke. I bugged out my eye at her to make her really scared, and then dumped a whole bunch of french fry in my orange bag. George and I had to store up in case Mrs. Buckworth wanted us to eat more mush. And . . . I had to save lots of food for the important day we'd run away.

Inside each of our boxes was a tiny plastic toy with green teeth and a head that bobbled back and forth. George and I poked the heads of our new toys over and over again.

As it turned out, Melons had about a hundred village markets.

There were markets for coffee and markets for ice cream and markets for flowers and markets for toys.

We stopped at a market that was just for Rooney and Puddles and bought them food, and then we stopped at an enormous market with nothing but people food.

Crazy.

In the people food market, giant icy coolers held mysterious frozen foods with pretty pictures. Lines of shelves held all sorts of other shiny foods that I'd never seen in my life. Mr. Buckworth would walk down a row and throw things in a big metal cart on wheels as George and I stood frozen in the same exact place staring at all the food.

American food didn't look like food because it was hidden in a box or in a plastic wrapper or in a can. Old Lady Suri at the bean stand would've been very upset to see her beans in a can. The chicken didn't look anything like a chicken because there were no feathers, and the vegetables had no bruises and bugs.

When Mr. Buckworth was busy itching his head about which box of milk to buy, and a kid stopped to stare at George's missing arm, I grabbed George's hand and whisked him around the corner. "Let's go, George."

"Where are we go—"

That's when we almost crashed into the girl. The same girl who'd been building the falling-down tower.

"Oh sorry," she said, and threw a can of something into her almost empty cart.

"That is . . . okay," I said.

She tripped on nothing and pushed her crooked pink glasses back up on her nose. I watched as she kept rolling her enormous cart down the aisle, looking up at the tall towers of food.

I turned back to George. "Now, you are Big Uncle."

"I am?"

"Yes." I found an empty cart and pushed it over to George. "And you are driving your Chevy taxi, as usual." George wheeled it back and forth with his hand. He stood on the back of the cart and made "achoo-achoo" sounds like the taxi's sick horn.

"Suddenly," I said dramatically, "your taxi hits a hot spot. Your tire explodes. BOOM!"

I knocked the cart into a pile of boxed food on a stand. It teetered and so did George.

"So you need a new job. But you don't care. You hate your taxi. You want to join the circus. You want to sell snacks like the black bottom monkeys. Coca-Cola and hot dog and french fry. 'Cause food is free." I took a box of something and a can of something off a shelf and stuck it in the new "backpack" that George's mommy had bought for him.

"It is?" George scrunched his eyes. "Are you sure, Babo?"

"In America it's free. You saw that girl? That food in her big basket? She's a kid, like you and me."

George nodded.

"So you don't have to worry." I spotted a plastic bag of noodle snakes and stuck it in my orange bag. "The leftover kids and Big Uncle are sick of being skin-'n'-bones skinny. In the circus you can be fat and full. Like Melons."

"Big Uncle is hungry." George poked his bony belly. He took more bags and cans and boxes off the shelf and stuffed them in his backpack. "Are kookies free too, Babo?"

"Kookies? Of course."

We immediately started searching for cookies. But it was hard to tell what was a cookie or not a cookie. Just as I was reaching into my orange bag for some of Mrs. Buckworth's leftover cookies, a big fat man in a uniform reached out and touched my shoulder. Mr. Buckworth touched George's backpack. Both of us jumped. When we drove home in the wagon Mr. Buckworth explained that food in America is definitely not free.

"Betti, you're not going to starve here . . ." said the Buckworths that night. "We're not sure . . . what you and George had to do in your country . . . survive . . . It's not okay to steal. Ever . . . If you want something . . . ask us, okay? We won't always be able to . . . give it to you . . . we'll try . . . have to believe . . . take care of you, sweetie . . ."

Lucy got bored with Mr. and Mrs. Buckworth's gobbledygook and said, "She understands already, Mom. Stealing is bad, Betti."

I nodded my head a whole bunch of times. "Stealing is bad. I am very, very, very bad."

Stealing was probably *so bad* that the Buckworths would ship me back immediately to the circus camp, but not on a ship. On a big bird airplane.

But before the Buckworths could even think about how horrible I was, Lucy said, "Dad, will you please tell us a story now?" She tilted her head and her ponytails tilted too. "In your bed?" And before Mr. Buckworth could answer, Lucy took my hand and led me to the Buckworths' big bedroom where we crawled into their big bed.

I loved stories! One story would be okay. The Buckworths didn't have to ship me off right away.

The dogs lay down on the floor. Mr. Buckworth got into bed on one side and Mrs. Buckworth sat up next to me on the other side. Lucy and I were smooshed between them like a hot dog or a cookie. It was almost like the circus camp, with all the leftover kids squished right up against me. But the Buckworths were Melons and we were in America.

"It's a slumber party!" squealed Lucy.

So Mr. Buckworth started telling Lucy and me a story from a book. It was about some poor girl who was a maid a long, long time ago.

"Is she a mermaid?" I asked.

"No, she's a girl, Betti." Lucy showed me a picture. "She's all dirty cause she cleans out the fireplace and dusts and stuff."

"Her name," Mr. Buckworth read dramatically, "is Cinderella."

"Is she a lion?" I asked. "Half a girl and half a lion? Named Cindi?"

Lucy turned to me, scrunched her eyes, and gave my arm a poke with her little finger. "Cinderella is just a plain old girl, Betti. Shhh."

So basically the rest of Mr. Buckworth's story from a book went like this: a Royal Prince came to Cindi's door with an invitation to a Royal Party at a Royal Palace. Cindi really wasn't invited because she was poor and dirty. But Cindi snuck in anyway because a ghost gave her special occasion clothes and shoes. She danced and danced with the Prince, until she tripped and her shoe flew off somewhere. The Prince came to Cindi's door with the missing shoe and he liked her shiny special occasion shoe so much that they got married. The Royal Prince was happy. The ghost was happy.

"But why does Cindi want to be Royal Princess and live in Royal Palace?" I asked. "It is lonely."

Lucy sighed. "*Because.* She can have anything she wants. The Prince *saved* her."

"Can circus people live there too? And the animals too?"

"No. It's a palace, Betti. A *palace.*"

Mr. Buckworth chuckled and closed his book. "So they lived happily ever after. Blah blah blah. The end."

"Now off to bed, girls," said Mrs. Buckworth. "Go on."

But Lucy already had her eyes closed. She let out a snort like a sleeping cow. Then she elbowed me under the covers, so I closed my eyes and let out a snort too.

Mrs. Buckworth sighed. "Just tonight, girls. You can sleep here tonight *only*." Soon the light went out and everyone was quiet.

From the dark I said, "I believe that . . . only American girls get saved."

MY EMPTY BOOK
(Days Four, Five, Six, in America)

Teeth paste = Horrible goo for teeth.

Pony tails = Tails sticking out of Lucy's red head.

Bi sikle = Sitting on wheels that ride.

Tree House = Hiding Place.

Mail Man = Man with mail.

Mail Boks = For new mail from Auntie Moo.

Skate bord = Like roller skates, but weirder.

Stop Sine = Red, must stop.

Moterr sikle = Like bicycle, but faster, with lady on it.

Garden = Flowers like Mrs. Buckworth's.

Dux = Quack quack

Pond = Like swamp, without green topping.

Porch = Falling down, with Melon circus girl in grass.

Busy-ness = People very, very busy doing ... I don't
know what.

French Fry = Yellow sticks to eat from France.

Hot Dog = Cooked dogs. Probably a tail.

Steal = Food not free.

Cindi Rella = Plain old dirty girl who is saved.

Happily Ever After = Blah blah blah. The end.

Summer Six

SUMMER IS THE best time of the whole year in America, because school is over and there's nothing to do. That's what Lucy told me after I'd been in America for a whole week.

"Sometimes I get bored, and sometimes I get in trouble," she said as we were walking on the white cement called "side walk." It didn't look like she was walking sideways to me. She told her mom that we definitely wanted to walk to Day Camp alone. No adults allowed. So Mr. Buckworth pretended that he wasn't walking with us, even though he was walking behind us with Rooney and Puddles.

Mrs. Buckworth said I didn't have to go to Day Camp if I didn't want to, but I was very excited to go to Day Camp! Maybe it was like the circus camp, at least a little. Maybe there were leftover kids. Even though Lenore, the adoption expert lady, said I'd adapt if I met some friends in America—and I definitely wasn't going to make friends or adapt—I was curious about Day Camp! Staying in America an extra day or two, just so I could go to Day Camp, wouldn't hurt anything.

Lucy stopped walking and set her backpack on the ground and bent down to tie her shoe. "Sometimes I watch TV all day, and then Mom gets mad and she makes me go outside."

I stopped too and set my orange bag on the ground. Mr. Buckworth had bought me a new pink backpack like Lucy's, but I told him that I already had a bag. Mine was better.

"So, this summer? Mom let me to go to Day Camp. So I don't drive her crazy. I guess that's why you get to go to Day Camp too. So you don't drive her crazy."

I suddenly imagined Lucy and me driving all over the place—in the wagon—like crazy people. "Drive crazy?" I asked her. "You mean, the wagon?"

Lucy laughed. "No, you silly. I can't drive 'til I'm sixteen. And I don't *want* to drive that stupid wagon. It's ugly. But I mean that when, I'm bored I bug my mom. I say, MOM! I'M BORED!"

"You *bug* . . . her?" These must've been the same words in my language for a little gnat that gave old people warts.

"I mean, my mom, she gets like this . . . wooooo . . ." Lucy twirled her finger around her head and made googley eyes. "Nuts. She says that if I'm bored it's my own fault. 'Cause I have an excellent imagination."

A magic nation? Nation meant a country, but I'd never heard of a magic country. And nuts? Mrs. Buckworth was like a peanut? My forehead got all wrinkled. I was trying to understand. I wanted to understand. But English was horribly difficult. And *Lucy English* was even worse.

Lucy sighed.

I sighed.

"Never mind," she said.

"Never mind," I said.

And we picked up the packs for our backs and kept walking to Day Camp without saying much at all.

"Welcome, Betti! We've been excited for you to join us!"

My good eye darted around nervously as I watched Mr. Buckworth leaving. He'd said, "You're going to be fine, little tiger." He put his hand on my head. "*Finally*, after a whole week of being with us, you'll get to have some fun with kids your own age."

He introduced me to Ms. Stacy, the Day Camp Teacher Lady, who introduced me to the other day campers: five of them sitting in a circle on the grass.

Ms. Stacy said she called them the Summer Five. Now, with me here, she could call us the Summer Six, which sounded much better. Ms. Stacy pointed for me to sit down in the circle.

"Can you all say hi to Betti?" she said.

"Hi," the campers muttered.

"Hello," I squeaked back in a tiny voice.

Lucy had left me to join her own Day Camp with the little kids. And George was sitting in another circle across the enormous play yard. He was in Day Camp too, and I could see him already giggling with an American girl. George looked like he'd been in Day Camp forever. Which just figured.

Day Camp happened at Betsy Ross Elementary School. And I'd also be going to Betsy Ross Elementary School in the fall, after the summer. That's what Lucy said. I'd be in the fifth grade unless I didn't know enough.

But I definitely knew enough and I wasn't going to be here after the summer anyway.

Lucy also told me that Betsy Ross was some lady who sewed up some flag for some American war a long, long time ago. I thought Lucy was making things up because it didn't seem as if there'd ever been a war in America. Everything looked too perfect and nothing was broken.

"You've all heard about Betti's country on TV," explained Camp Lady Stacy.

She pulled a map out of her camp box on the grass. She pointed to my country and all the campers leaned forward trying to see it. I tried to see it too. My home was tiny next to all sorts of huge countries. It was light green and shaped like a chicken liver.

"We've all seen pictures of the war . . ."

The campers kept squinting at Ms. Stacy's map, and then at me. At the map, then at me. At the same time, I was looking at them. They all had different colored skin. Pink melon to charcoal black and everything in between. Old Lady Suri never told me that Melons came in different colors.

"We've seen the news, and we've heard about our soldiers too, right? Maybe some of you even know a soldier who's over there . . ."

It was weird hearing a Melon talk about my country. I wondered what exactly they'd all heard, what pictures they'd seen. Maybe they saw pretty people having a happy vacation, just like the Buckworths' book.

I watched the girl's mouth on the other side of the circle. She was chewing gum, chewing chewing, like the pigs in the pig yard. She had pointy hair with little pink streaks. Did it grow like that? That hair was crazier than mine and Sister Baroo would be very upset to comb out hair like that.

There was a boy in the circle with freckles and funny wires on his teeth, and two other boys wearing hats, but the hats were accidentally turned backward on their heads. The fifth camper was a round Melon girl with a pink face. She was tapping the toes of her play shoes together over and over again. Tap tap tap.

"Betti? Would you like to tell us anything about your life back home? You can tell us yourself. I'm afraid I don't know nearly enough." Ms. Stacy blushed.

For a second I forgot about the chewing and the tapping and the wire teeth. I tried hard to picture the circus camp: me climbing the tallest trees so I could see everything. I was definitely the leader and I definitely had a Big Mouth. But here? I could hardly spit out a single word.

"I lived . . . I live . . . at . . . people food market."

"At the market?" Ms. Stacy looked very confused.

The kids just laughed.

"I mean I live . . ." The words were coming out all wrong. I couldn't think straight. "At airport. At Base Mint. No . . ." I inhaled a big breath and thought I'd faint face-first. "I live at circus."

"At the circus?" Ms. Stacy started speaking very slowly, as if I had an out-of-order brain. "Do you mean—"

"I live at circus!" I said louder. "That is where I live!"

The girl with the crazy hair and the gum said, "The *circus?*"

"What circus?" asked a backward-hat boy with a horrible smirk.

"Fifi . . . the elephant . . . has clowns on back. Taller than mountain." I pointed up. "Big, big birds speak . . . words in languages. Three. Puppet Man with little head"—I held out my hand as if a head was nestled there—"do show. About soldiers. Smooshed. By Fifi. And people laugh."

The campers stared.

"And—and—" I was sure they were looking at my bad eye. They probably thought I was making things up.

The leftover kids *always* believed me.

My face was hot. I think I had sweat dripping from the top of my head down through my hair.

The other boy with a backward hat let out a snickering snort and poked his friend.

My new overalls were making me itch and I looked down at my horribly new American play shoes. "Story is over," I squeaked. "Blah blah blah. The end."

"That's all right," said Camp Lady Stacy. "No worries, Betti. Maybe tomorrow."

Dude and Brown Bag Food.

IT WAS A long day at Day Camp.

And nothing at all like my circus camp.

Camp Lady Stacy told me that she was a brand-new teacher. She would be a real teacher as soon as school started in the fall, after she practiced being a teacher in Day Camp. She said that we were her first "guinea pigs." She laughed and the campers laughed too.

I didn't understand what was so funny about Ms. Stacy calling us pigs.

So instead of listening to Ms. Stacy, I looked around at all the funny things: the funny American trees, and the campers' funny clothes, and the weird games where kids swung ropes over their heads and climbed on colored things that came out of the ground like enormous bugs. Funny, but not nearly as fun as the circus camp.

Then my eye landed on something familiar. Someone. All the way across the play yard I saw a girl sitting
on a bench. It was the same girl I had seen sitting on
the porch of the tilted house, building the tower, shopping at the people food market. The girl who reminded
me of a circus girl, even though she was a Melon.

This time there was an old, old lady sitting next to
her. The old lady's hand was on the girl's knee and the
girl was leaning against her. They were talking softly,
smiling, with a big book open on their laps. It made me
think of Auntie Moo and me.

My good eye got watery and I started to sniffle, but
that was when Ms. Stacy said it was time for lunch. The
Summer Five took brown bags out of their backpacks,
so I took my brown bag out of my orange bag. Mrs.
Buckworth had handed it to me before I left this morning. Inside there was an apple fruit and a cookie and two
pieces of uncooked bread with jelly and brown nutty
goo smudged inside. I said "ick" and "yummy" and ate
it all in about one second, even if it tasted funny.

But the other campers?

The boy named Timmy, with wire teeth, accidentally
spit food out of his mouth and wiped his shirt with a
tissue. The girl named Sam, with streaky hair, doodled
strange creatures on her paper bag, and the pink Melon
girl named Tabitha talked to Ms. Stacy about her cat.
The two backward-hat boys, Jerry and Bobby Ray, kept

calling each other "dude." They laughed like crazy and punched each other's arms.

I wasn't sure what "dude" meant. I thought maybe it was their last name, and maybe the backward-hat boys were brothers. Maybe dude meant a sock in the arm, or maybe it meant "friend." If it meant friend, I knew they'd never call me dude.

During food time all the campers talked and talked and laughed. Sometimes they looked at me, but usually they ignored me.

Once I heard one of the boys with a backward hat quietly say, "Does the new girl with the eye understand anything?"

The other boy answered, "No clue, dude."

After that I pretended that my ears were out of order.

The Summer Five ate their cookies fast, without even saying "ick." When Ms. Stacy told us that we could go and play, they left half of their bread and half of their fruit and half of their weird boxed juice just sitting there on plastic bags.

I snatched three goopy bread squares, two fruits, and one half-juice. I drank the juice in one slurp. And the rest of it? Well, I stuffed all of it into my orange bag.

When Ms. Stacy told us to throw our leftovers in the trash, there were no more leftovers. No one even seemed to notice because they were all focused on Ms.

Stacy's next "fun activiteee": something called "Kick Ball."

I asked Sam, the girl with pointy hair, "What does it mean?"

"What does what mean?"

"Kick Ball?"

She stared at me and squinted her eyes. "It means that you *kick* the *ball*. And run. No biggie."

Kick Ball sounded very boring compared to my games.

So I nudged Sam and said, "Now . . . you be Cindi. She sing in cage. Not zoo. She miss her love. Boy lion."

Sam turned to me and snapped her blue gum. "*What?*"

I put my nose in the air and walked over to Timmy. I tugged on the back of his shirt. "You . . . be Snake Lady. She live in tree." I pointed over at a funny tree. "She speak snake. Ssssss."

Timmy tilted his head and licked his wire teeth lips. "I don't understand, Betti."

Tabitha didn't understand either when I told her, "You be Fifi the elephant. She has big feet and big nose. You dance."

"I'm not an elephant. That's mean!" Tabitha's nose quivered and she blinked a whole bunch of times.

I wanted to play with George instead.

"George!" I hollered across the play yard, waving my arms around. "George! George!"

George didn't even hear me. He was too busy with the second graders making funny hats and squealing as if this was the most fun he'd ever had in his whole life.

George was wearing the most ugly hat I'd ever seen. His extra-large ears stuck out like bananas on a vine.

But it was too late for my good games anyway. Kids were already kicking the ball, running across the grass, running around in circles, catching the ball or picking it up, and bombing it at someone all over again. A girl got hit straight in the knee, so she hobbled off the playground crying. Kickball made me dizzy.

"Go! Go!" and "Whoo hoo!" and "Run!" they hollered and clapped as if kickball was some great circus act.

Suddenly someone pushed me to the front of a line. I watched my bright white play shoes as the ball came barreling toward me on the grass.

Three . . .

Two . . .

One . . .

KICK!

The campers all reached their arms up, they jumped a little, their eyes all peered up and squinted from the sun as my ball flew through the sky. They looked just like the leftover kids when there was a Melon plane flying over the circus camp.

And me? I ran like crazy. I wasn't sure where I was supposed to run exactly, so I ran straight toward George.

"GEORGE!" I shouted.

The voices behind me were shouting, "Get her!" and "Where is she going?" as I ran straight past all of them.

It was the perfect time to run away. Just perfect. I was going to run and run and run and run.

"Hurry, George!" I shouted, but George was too busy playing with his hat.

That's when I realized that someone was chasing me. "I'm not afraid of you," I whispered between jagged breaths. I was known for being the fastest runner in the whole circus camp, maybe the whole village, even with my missing toes. But there weren't any places to hide in the play yard. No woods. No trees. No swamps.

The ball whizzed right past me, and right past George's ear.

"I GOT HER!" shouted the dude Bobby Ray. "On the shoulder."

I stopped running and swung around. "NO . . . YOU . . . DID NOT!"

"I DID TOO!" His hands were clenched tight as he hit them against his sides. His brown hair was hanging over his eyes and I thought that his backward hat might fall off.

"YOU'RE OUT!"

I didn't know what it meant to be "out." I wasn't sure if it was a good thing or a bad thing to be out.

So I kicked Bobby Ray.

"OW! She kicked me!" Bobby Ray rubbed his bottom, exactly where I'd kicked him. "Ms. Stacy! She—"

Running away was more dangerous than I thought.

So there was really only one place to go.

No one ever messed with old ladies in my country. They were the special ones. Everyone held their breath when old ladies told their stories. Old ladies had seen just about everything. They could see all the way into the past and halfway into the future.

No one would ever hit an old lady with a ball.

I ran right behind the girl who was sitting on the bench with the old, old lady. I gripped the back of the bench with my hands until they turned white. I was breathing straight into the back of their heads. Their hair blew up and down. The old lady's hair was a tropical blue color, which matched her blue-veined hands. The girl stopped reading.

"Hi," she said, turning around and looking up at me. Her eyes were squinting behind her crooked pink glasses.

"Nice of you to join us, sweet girl," said the old, old lady. She didn't look at me because she was staring straight ahead in her dark gray glasses.

"Those games get nasty." The girl motioned with her head toward the kickball game. "I'm always the first one out."

I nodded. Nasty. Which must've been the Melon word for when a ghost got mad and gave a bad kid purple pimples.

"I'm Mayda," said the girl, smiling just a little. "And this is Nanny. We're reading. You can listen, if you want."

Nanny patted a place on the bench next to her, just as the kickball bounced toward the bench and landed between Nanny's brown slipper shoes. Camp Lady Stacy was waving like crazy to me across the play yard.

It was the end of kickball and the end of Day Camp.

I'd have to run away on another day—I'd just have to wait—because I didn't want to move an inch. I wanted to sit right there on the bench next to Mayda and Nanny. Mayda watched the campers for a second, and then she turned to the next page of her big book. Nanny put her wrinkled hand on the new page to keep it from flipping over.

Mayda took a breath and was about to start reading, when I suddenly blurted out, "My name is Babo. Betti. Betti Babo. You can call me Betti. Mrs. Buckworth's mama. It maybe is easier."

Roller Derby Lucy

IT IS BAD to kick people.

I told Mrs. Buckworth exactly how bad I was. Bobby Ray was a very good boy playing kickball, I told Mrs. Buckworth, but I was a very bad girl. Because I wanted to kick him in the bottom. For no good reason. That's just how I am. Horrible.

I was all ready for Mrs. Buckworth to tell me to pack up my orange bag because I'd be flying straight back to the circus camp. Immediately.

Instead, she said I was . . . grounded.

"Grownded?" Being grounded sounded horrible!

No TV for the rest of the day. No swinging on the swinging seats in the yard. I had to play quietly in my room. That's what Mrs. Buckworth said.

I scrunched my face. "Only . . . one *day*?"

"Betti," she said, "you're not a bad girl. I know better than that."

"Yes I am." I shook my head lots of times. "Bad bad."

"No, I think there must've been a reason that you kicked Bobby Ray." Mrs. Buckworth tilted her head and looked straight into my eyes. "Still, you're absolutely right. It's not nice to kick anybody. For any reason. And because you're smart enough to know that already, well then, you're grounded for today. I'm sorry."

I sighed.

First I sat in my yellow room and ate some leftover lunch out of my orange bag. Then I drew some horrible pictures for Auntie Moo in my Empty Book. Mean backward hats, and wire teeth, and a pig mouth, and crazy spiked hair, and me kicking a bad boy. I also wrote down important new words like "drive me crazy," and "nuts," and "dude." Auntie Moo would want to know these words too. I read her letter again and folded it up neatly.

I changed out of my Day Camp clothes, back into my circus dress, and stood in front of the mirror. I pretended I was the Snake Lady. "Ssssss. Ssssss." I swayed back and forth to a rattlesnake rhythm. I pretended that I was the Hairy Bear Boy. I beat my chest and squinted my eyes and put my nose right up to the glass. I pretended I was Santy Claws and the Fairy Ghost with

Teeth. I growled and scratched and chomped my fangs like a little tiger.

Then I got on top of my bed and put my arms out and put one foot in front of the other. My line in the sky. I had to practice every second so those Melon campers would believe me. I did live at the circus. I am a circus star. I watched my feet as I walked to the end of my bouncy bed, and—

"Betti?"

I tripped on my pillow and tipped over.

Lucy tilted her head and stared at me. One of her ponytails was practically on top of her head and the other was way down by her shoulder. Her play pants had big circles of dirt on the knees. "What are you doing, Betti?"

"I am playing."

"Playing *what*?"

I opened my mouth really wide. "I am playing that a lady ghost watch me and try to steal my teeth."

"Oh," said Lucy.

"Then . . . an important ghost man with claws come down from sky." I pointed at my ceiling. "He only come one time in year—today. But they are not my mama and dad."

"Well, can I play too?" Lucy didn't wait for an answer. She came and sat down right next to me.

"I am bad. I am grounded."

"Sometimes I'm bad too. Really, really bad. I get grounded all the time." Lucy bounced on the bed, which made me bounce too. "But I don't want to play that game with the teeth lady or the man with claws." In about one second Lucy ran out of my room hollering, "I know!" And then came leaping back. "Look, Betti! Look what I have!"

Lucy's little hand was gripping a doll with wheels on her shoes. "Her name is . . . Roller Derby Tina. She's my very favorite . . . I never even play with her 'cause . . . don't want her to get dirty . . . or to . . ."

Gobbledygook.

Lucy held her doll up in front of my nose so I had to look at her up close.

"Rolling Derby Teeena. She is like . . . picture."

"What picture?"

I got up and opened my secret door closet. I took out my orange bag and dug to the bottom for the picture. Lucy with wheels on her feet.

"Oh!" Lucy beamed. "That's me roller-skating!"

"It is . . . fun?"

"It is *so* fun. I love to skate. And I'm *so* good, Betti. You should see me! Sometimes I roller-skate outside, and sometimes Dad takes me to the roller rink. He's not as good as me though. I'm probably the best skater in the world." Lucy started to twirl around my yellow room. Then she lifted one leg and bounced around and put her arms out like an exotic bird.

Once in a while Lucy did something interesting. I really needed to practice for the circus, but instead I said, "I want to play that."

"Well, Dad said that I can't skate unless I skate with him. It's kinda dangerous, he says. But maybe we can just try them on."

Dangerous? Perfect.

"Okay. Yes." And just as I said it, Lucy was out the door in a flash. When she came back she had two pairs of roller skates in her hands, one tiny red pair and one enormous blue and white striped pair. Lucy held out the big pair for me as she took off her play shoes and laced up the red skates on her feet.

I took the huge wheel shoes in my hands and looked at them. I rolled one of them up and over my orange bag and along the edge of my bed. They were about as long as my arm. "My wheel shoes are too big."

Lucy was already trying to roll around on the floor. "Yeah, they're my dad's. Just put some socks in 'em."

I balled up some of my new white socks, stuffed them inside the huge skates, and slipped the skates on. They felt like someone else's feet, but I didn't care. My missing toes never felt much anyway.

"It's kinda hard at first." Lucy giggled, holding on to my arm.

I tried to roll. It was like walking in the pig yard, heavy and sloppy. But I felt so tall. Like a giant! The tallest girl in the world! Like my mama!

"Let's go outside," I said.

Lucy looked toward the door. "We're not supposed to." She shuffled her skating feet. "Mom'll get mad. We're supposed to stay here while she's working in her office."

Perfect. I was grounded, so I was supposed to play inside. But I had to make Mrs. Buckworth really, really mad. Maybe it was even possible to run away on roller skates, like a circus star. To roll and roll and roll and roll away. "Just for one minute?"

"Well, I guess a minute is okay. We have to be quiet though. Okay, Betti?"

I nodded and threw my orange bag over my shoulder, and then we tiptoed into the hallway in our roller skates. I clunked behind Lucy, holding on to the wall. My circus dress was getting all clumped up around my knees. Rooney woke up from his nap on the sofa and Puddles stretched and itched herself. We passed a door that was open a crack. Lucy looked back at me and said "Shhhh," but I had to peek inside.

Mrs. Buckworth was sitting in front of a machine that stared out like a strange square face. Her hands were moving fast. And then they stopped. She sighed and mumbled things to herself and chewed on a pencil. And then her hands moved fast again. Click click click.

Mrs. Buckworth didn't even notice as Lucy and

I slipped out the front door and hobbled down the front steps. Lucy was already ahead of me, rolling back and forth down the sidewalk, with Roller Derby Tina clutched tightly in one hand. "Look at me," she tried to squeal quietly. "Watch me, Betti!"

I wanted to go faster. Step step, roll roll, but Lucy had no idea how clumsy I was in my own country. Rooney kept biting at the jaggedy threads on the bottom of my circus dress, which made things worse. My hands swatted at the air. "Shoo, shoo!"

Lucy skated around in circles; she went toward the sidewalk and over the cracks. "Betti, watch this!" She held one foot up and then the other.

We skated down the cement path to where the Buckworths' yard ended. Then we kept going, down the block past all the houses that looked like the Buckworths' house. I felt happy for a second, rolling away. Unfortunately I didn't know that the sidewalk was a small hill. And we were rolling down. Not much, just a little. But my rolling feet started to move on their own.

Faster . . .

And faster . . .

And then even faster . . .

When Lucy saw me, her mouth made a little "o" as my arms started waving in huge circles. "Wait, Betti!" I heard her scream. "Wait for me!" She skated super fast to catch up and her free hand reached out for mine. Finally . . . she grabbed it. Her fingers squeezed my hand.

Rooney caught us too, and Puddles was barking like crazy.

"Help!" I said, but I was too late and my voice was too small. "Help," I tried again. "Help! HELP!"

"Helllllllp!" Lucy squealed, as if we were *playing*, as if she'd never had so much fun in her whole life.

"HOLD ON, GIRLS!" A voice suddenly called behind us. "I'M COMING!"

Lucy and I were probably going faster than an airplane. My hair was flying and so were Lucy's ponytails. Rooney's ears flopped and flapped as we flew past trees and yards, and we dodged a lady walking with a pink baby.

"EEEEEEEEEK!"

I made a flying leap. Lucy had to fly with me because her hand was attached to mine. We landed in a jungle. My head was on a dirt mound, and tall grass was all around us.

Perfect quiet. It was as if I'd flown straight home to my country.

"Betti Babo? Are you okay?"

Then I saw the thick pink glasses and the knotty hair. Mayda was holding a plastic blue dog in her hands and she looked like a giant. "Hold on, Betti!" She disappeared and I heard her holler to the porch next door, "Nanny!"

"Girls! Are you okay?" Mrs. Buckworth's face was hovering over us.

"Are they okay?" Nanny called out as she inched her way over to us in her slipper shoes.

My enormous roller skates had flown off and disappeared into Mayda's jungle grass. Roller Derby Tina's head had flown off too.

One of my arms had a little blood on it. It hurt, a little, but at least now Mrs. Buckworth would really know that she picked the wrong leftover kid. Betti gets in trouble even when she's grounded. Betti probably broke something else. Betti probably lost more toes or poked out her good eye. Horrible.

But it turned out that Mrs. Buckworth wasn't mad at me. She was worried about Lucy. Lucy was crying and whimpering and holding her leg against her chest. "Ow ow ow ow ow ow."

It wasn't supposed to go this way at all. I was supposed to get in big trouble but I wasn't supposed to make Lucy broken.

Another Broken Kid

"HOSPEE TALL."

That's where Lucy had to go. That is where broken people get fixed.

Mayda found the lost roller skates, and my orange bag, and the doll head in her grass, while Mrs. Buckworth took Lucy's skate off her foot, which was suddenly fat and ugly.

Nanny told Mrs. Buckworth that they'd watch out for me while Mrs. Buckworth took Lucy to the hospital.

"It's no trouble," said Nanny. "We're quite fond of Babo Betti. We met her at Day Camp."

"I want to teach her English," said Mayda.

Mrs. Buckworth looked at Mayda, and then at Nanny, and then at me. Totally confused. "Well, okay. If you're absolutely sure."

"Of course," said Nanny.

"Okay," I said. Because I was afraid that Mrs. Buckworth would make me go to the hospital too. I did not want to get fixed.

I stood in the tall grass and checked my circus dress for damage. Only a few new small holes and a green streak down the arm from grass. After Mrs. Buckworth took Lucy to the hospital, Mayda walked toward her house and looked over her shoulder. "Don't you want to come in, Betti?"

I sucked in my breath. "Okay."

So the three of us, Mayda and Nanny and I, walked slower than turtles up Mayda's porch steps. There was an old crooked swing on the porch and a dead plant in a can. When Mayda opened the front door I was afraid that it might fall off, like the door on Big Uncle's taxi.

The inside of Mayda's house was small and everything looked like it was about a hundred years old. Nothing looked fluffy like the Buckworths' house. The sofa didn't match the pillows. It had holes in it and some metal wires stuck up from the bottom. The fluffy stuff on the floor didn't look like grass at all. It was stained, and there were pictures on the walls but the pictures all looked faded and lopsided. I didn't even see a TV anywhere!

I loved Mayda's house!

Mayda gave me some flip-flops to put on, and Nanny

had me sit on a chair in the kitchen. Mayda got a wet warm cloth and wiped off the spot of blood. Nanny ran her old wrinkled hand gently over my arm and put some medicine on my wound.

"Oh, I'm sorry, sweet girl, if this stings." Nanny put a plastic square on my arm that stuck. "It's not more than a scrape, but it'll sure be sore for the night." Then she patted my arm and said: "Now, how about helping Mayda and me bake some cookies? Cookies might be just what the doctor ordered."

I wondered if the doctor ordered Lucy to get cookies too. Maybe that was an American cure to make her better. I hoped she was eating a lot of cookies so she wouldn't die.

I got to crack three eggs into a bowl. Mayda dropped in little pieces of dark candy called "choclit chips." We both put in flour and took turns stirring. Mayda had flour all over her face but I tried not to giggle. We dropped balls of cookie onto a pan and then Mayda said we got to lick our spoons. Ick. Yummy.

Then Mayda and Nanny started asking questions about my country. I didn't know how they even knew about my country, or how they knew that I came from my country. But somehow they did.

"Nanny and I have read all about it in the newspaper. We read every day."

"Absolutely horrible!" Nanny clenched her wrinkled,

spotty hands and her face turned sad. Or mad. It was hard to say.

"Yeah." Mayda nodded. "It sounds so dangerous."

"It is not bad." I shrugged, even though I was thinking about the BOOMS and hiding in the dark. "It is very, very beautiful. I live on a big . . . moterr sickle."

Mayda looked confused. "A motorcyle?"

"I mean, palace. My dad is Royal Prince. He is green."

"Goodness," said Nanny.

"Green?" asked Mayda.

"And . . . I am just . . . on a trip. A tour." I tried very hard to show a fake smile like the pretty people in the Buckworths' book about my country. "Here. In America."

"A trip? Really? You're going *back there*?" Mayda's mouth was wide open.

"The war . . . will end," I told her. "After summer. Summer is best time in whole year."

"*This* summer? After so many years? Well, I certainly hope so," Nanny said.

I didn't want to talk about it anymore.

Fortunately that's when Mayda handed me a cookie and a cup of milk. I took a long time chewing my manure patty so I wouldn't have to answer their hard questions. I said "Ick" and "Yummy."

Nanny shook her head sadly. "Well, we'll miss you

after the summer if you go back home. We certainly will."

Mayda sighed. "Yeah, I thought you might be in the fifth grade with me. When school starts."

"Mayda's going to be a new student at Betsy Ross Elementary."

Mayda looked at her feet. She played with her fingers. She didn't look happy about being a new student. Not happy at all. "Yeah. Another new school." She rolled her eyes and looked into space. "Ugh."

Which must've been the word for when you get the locked lip sickness and you can't talk anymore.

Nanny was knitting a green and yellow sock. She patted a spot on the sofa for Mayda and me to sit next to her.

Mayda sat down, and I was starting to sit down too, but I tripped over a big pile of books next to the sofa and stubbed my toes.

"Oh! Are you okay, Betti?" asked Mayda. "Sorry, our house is kind of messy. My dad and I don't have much time to clean."

"That is okay. I like messy. My country is messy."

Mayda smiled, just a little. She didn't care about the mess either. Not really.

"It is my eye." I pointed at my fish eye as I sat down right between them. "Sometimes my eye makes me fall. It is very broken."

Nanny touched my knee with her hundred-year-old

wrinkly hand. "Oh, I'm in the same boat, Betti! My eyes. I'm practically blind as a bat!"

I didn't know what boats and bats had to do with being blind, but I nodded.

"No." Mayda smiled at me. "I think Nanny secretly sees things better than most people, Betti."

"Well, I do have a good imagination, that's true." Nanny tapped my knee. "Even though my eyes don't work, I'm sure that my imagination sees things better than they really are. Maybe that's the same with you, Betti. With your eye? I think that colors are brighter in my bad ol' eyes. Reds are redder and greens are greener. And the sun shines most of the time, even on rainy days."

Nanny stared off into space as if she was looking at something very important. Her eyes were milky and they didn't even blink.

That's when I knew that Nanny had a magic nation, where the sun shined all the time.

"Do you know what's weird?" Mayda said to me. "Nanny says that she knows exactly what I look like even though she can't really see me."

"I know that you're a very beautiful girl."

"Ha! You're so wrong!"

Mayda and Nanny laughed a private laugh, just like Auntie Moo and I used to laugh.

My good eye got watery. Suddenly I dug around in

my orange bag and found my Empty Book. My letter from Auntie Moo fell on the floor. I quickly picked it up, dusted it off, and returned it to its important place on the last page. I opened my book on my lap, and Mayda and Nanny leaned in to see.

Mayda pointed to the very first picture. "It's a very tall woman, Nanny," explained Mayda. "And she has a tail."

Nanny put her hand on my picture as if she was seeing everything: the circus lights, and the smell of the trees. The sounds and the colors and my mama.

"A tail? My goodness!" exclaimed Nanny. "You do see very pretty things with your eyes, don't you, sweet girl. A marvelous imagination!"

My face turned pink. I really wanted a marvelous magic nation, just like Nanny!

Mayda carefully turned the pages. "What's this, Betti?"

"It is a . . . Merrr-made. And many shoes."

"How 'bout this one?"

"It is a fairy pulling out teeth."

Mayda smiled.

"This is a teeny-tiny puppet head. In my hand."

Mayda nodded and thought about things. Then she pointed.

"And this is . . . mush. Mrs. Buckworth made mush. I said 'ick' and 'yummy' and ate it all."

Mayda and Nanny laughed, nice laughs, and I had to smile too, just a little.

Then Mayda ran to the kitchen. She rummaged through a whole bunch of mess on the table and ran back with a colored pen. Starting at the very beginning, she wrote new words in my Empty Book next to my old words.

Empty Book
Microwave
Refrigerator
Kitchen
Television or TV
Living Room
Basement
Mermaid

It was almost like when Auntie Moo gave me English lessons.

Cookie.

"Koooky?" I repeated.

"Cookie," said Mayda. Then she wrote: "Betti likes to eat cookies."

I took a big bite of my chocolate chip cookie, and smiled with puffed-out cheeks. "Yummy."

Mayda taught me lots of new words, and lots of new sentences on paper. "Fifth grade" and "Betti is visiting America," and "Betti hopes the war ends soon," and "Mayda hopes that Betti stays here so they can be friends." I asked Mayda how to spell some very important sentences too, like "Betti thinks that America is too big," and "America is crazy." These sentences made Mayda and Nanny laugh a lot.

Auntie Moo was my school, but I didn't think it would hurt if Mayda taught me just a little. Just for now.

Fat Feet and Disco

MR. BUCKWORTH CAME to pick me up in the wagon and drove me back to the Buckworths' house. He made me something called "peeeza" in the oven. Pizza was round and cut up in slivers like pieces of the moon. I ate lots of slivers, but Rooney and Puddles liked pizza even more because they chomped half the box when Mr. Buckworth wasn't looking.

Mr. Buckworth told me about his day as Vice President and he asked me questions about Day Camp. "Are the kids nice? How do you like Ms. Stacy? Did you do anything fun, Betti?"

I took a deep breath and began: "Ms. Stacy, she said I was a pig. A boy has bars on his teeth, like this." I put my fingers in my mouth so I could show Mr. Buckworth big scary fangs. "There is dudes with hats.

We play kickball. But my games is better. Cindi and Snake Lady, but girl named Tabitha say, 'I am not an elephant.' She get mad because I am very mean girl. Then I kick ball and dude say, 'You are *out*.' So I was very, very horrible, Mr. Buckworth. I kick dude. No reason. I get grounded. And then . . . I was very bad again because I make Lucy roller-skate. I say, 'Let's go outside.' She got broken. It is because of me. Horrible."

Mr. Buckworth's eyebrows tilted and he itched his head..

"And I got broken too." That's when I held out my wounded arm.

Mr. Buckworth made a *tsk tsk* sound. "Roller skates . . ." He shook his head as he looked at my tiny scratch up close. "They're pretty fun, aren't they? But they cause some bad accidents."

I nodded. I was all ready for Mr. Buckworth to tell me that he wanted to choose another leftover kid. Immediately.

Instead, he said, "It's not your fault that Lucy got hurt, Betti. Don't think that. But, you girls *definitely* need to have one of us with you while you're skating, okay? From now on?"

I sighed.

Then Mr. Buckworth forgot about horrible me in about one second, and he got a little smile on his face.

"Did Lucy tell you that your mom and I used to disco skate when we were your age?"

I scrunched my eyes. "What is 'disss-ko'?"

"Like this." Mr. Buckworth danced around the kitchen as if he had baby mice in his fancy bank suit. Laughing, he grabbed my hand and made me disco too. My feet were clunky as he twirled me around the table and waved his arms all over the place and hummed some strange disco song. Mr. Buckworth was sort of funny.

And definitely crazy.

While we were pointing our fingers at the ceiling and shaking our hips, the front door opened with Lucy in Mrs. Buckworth's arms. Lucy's foot was wrapped in a brown cloth and it looked about five times bigger than her other foot.

"She's sound asleep, poor thing," whispered Mrs. Buckworth.

The Buckworths walked into Lucy's pink room and laid Lucy in her bed. I followed, and so did the dogs.

"What did the doctor say?" asked Mr. Buckworth.

"It's a sprain," answered Mrs. Buckworth.

I had no idea what a sprain was, but it sounded horrible.

Everyone I knew was broken, and now Lucy was broken too.

Soon I walked to my yellow room and slid my Empty

Book out from under my pillow. I had to draw before I forgot anything: a kickball with a jaggedy frown face. A doll with no head. Flying girls. My bloody wounded arm. Auntie Moo would definitely be worried. She'd understand everything. I touched her letter in the back of my book. I wished she could see the world as I was seeing it.

After I finished picture number five—Lucy looking like a freaky monster with an elephant foot—the Buckworths tapped softly on my door and poked their heads in.

"Betti?"

I slipped my book back under my pillow.

"Are you okay, little tiger?"

I probably looked like a ghost. Dangerous America.

"What's the matter, sweetie?"

I gulped. "Is Lucy going to . . . die?"

"Die?" Mr. Buckworth chuckled and then he stopped when he realized that I was very, very serious. "Oh no, Betti. Her foot's going to be just fine. She'll be up walking around in a couple of days." He plopped his hand on my head, and looked at me up close. "Please don't worry, little tiger."

The Buckworths had no idea that I was *always* worried.

I took a deep breath. "When circus kids go down to my village, I not sure, I don't know if they will come home. They may step on snake, or catch a sick that make their bones go green, or disappear in river or in poof of smoke. I am afraid for Auntie Moo. And I worry that she disappear too and we will be leftover. Again."

Worry probably got under my skin the day the circus camp burned. It was inside of me, just like water.

"Now . . ."—my voice was barely a squeak—"I worry about Lucy."

"Oh sweetie, of course you're worried." Mrs. Buckworth put her arms around me.

I played with my fingers. I picked up my one-eyed doll and set her in my lap.

"I hope your friends at the camp will be okay, Betti. I really do," said Mr. Buckworth. He looked off into space as if he was looking at something very important. "And Auntie Moo too."

Mrs. Buckworth looked sad and smoothed out my hair with her hand.

"Now . . . as for Lucy?" Mr. Buckworth continued, "I can promise you she'll be okay. I promise."

I wanted to believe that promises from the Buckworths were good, just like Auntie Moo's promises.

Mr. Buckworth leaned over and kissed me on my cheek and Mrs. Buckworth kissed me on my forehead.

"Have sweet dreams, sweetie," said Mrs. Buckworth.

"Even if you may not love *us* quite yet, little tiger," said Mr. Buckworth, turning out the light, "we still love you."

I touched my cheek and fell asleep.

IN THE MIDDLE of the night I shot straight up in my bed. Not-so-sweet dreams. I grabbed for my potato sack on top of my pillow and clenched it tight in my hand. Then I threw my blanket off my bed and it landed on Rooney.

I put my bare feet down on the floor and felt for the fake grass with my toes. I walked softly out of my yellow room and into the hall. Rooney and Puddles followed me. Straight to the pink room.

I pushed open Lucy's door and tiptoed in. I sat on the floor with my elbows on her pink bed and stared into her face. She looked just like a doll. Like Roller Derby Tina. I poked her to make sure she was still alive and, sure enough, her chest was moving up and down.

This wasn't the way it was supposed to happen at all. I was supposed to be the broken one in America. Not the leader. Because I had a terrible time leaving sprained kids.

I took a deep breath and began: *"There is a beautiful girl who roll like crazy on rolling skates. She is sooooo fast that clowns with red hair cannot touch her. The elephant has very big rolling skates, and the lion skates around the lion cage. The beautiful girl laughs, and the clowns and the animals laugh, and no one ever falls down. . . ."*

It was harder telling a Big Mouth story in English. I had to stop and think of words and start again. I had to move my hands all over the place to explain what I meant, even though Lucy's eyes were still closed.

After I finished the story, I whispered: "Do not die, Lucy. Do not die, please?"

Even if Lenore, the adoption expert lady, said that I'd adapt once I got used to things in America—and I was definitely not going to adapt—I was used to watching over the leftover kids at the circus camp. And now I had to watch over Lucy. To make sure she was okay. Even if I had to stay another day.

I had planned to give all of my scary pictures to Auntie Moo, but instead I ripped one out of my special book. I laid it on the pillow next to Lucy's nose.

MY EMPTY BOOK
(One WEEK in America)

Summmer = Nothing to do.
Drive crazy = Go crazy, but not in car.
You bug her = A gnat will give warts to Mrs.
　　Buckworth. Must go to Day Camp.
Nuts = Mrs. Buckworth is a peanut?

A Magic Nation = A nation where people aren't bored.
  And see sun.

Gineee pigs = Ms. Stacy thinks I am a pig?

Doood = Brother? Friend? Punch in arm? Not me.

You are out = Not good. Run!

Kickball = Kick the ball, not the boy.

Nasteee = The ghosts giving another bad kid purple
  pimples.

Day Camp = <u>Not</u> like the Circus Camp.

Mayda and Nanny = Like Auntie Moo and me.

Grownded = In big trouble.

Roller Skating = Wheels on shoes, rolling down.

Hospee tall = Tall building where broken people get fixed.

Choclit Chips = Brown candies in cookies.

Betti likes to eat cookies.

Fifth grade.

Betti is visiting America.

Betti hopes the war ends soon.

Betti thinks that America is too big.

America is crazy.

Peeeza = Chewy slivers, like pieces of moon.

Disss-ko = Mr. Buckworth dancing like crazy.

Sprain = Lucy is very broken.

The Hiding Place

"I LOVE MY picture, Betti! See?"

Lucy pointed over her head. It was the next morning and my scary monster picture of her was taped above her bed in the pink room. It looked even scarier hanging on the wall. "We don't get to go to Day Camp today." She was sitting up, smiling her no-teeth smile. "Because I'm hurt." The TV had been moved into her room and the happy/sad people's voices were blasting. "But GUESS WHAT? Mom said we could have sugar cereal this morning. As a special treat. 'Cause usually we only get it on Saturdays. What kind of cereal do you like, Betti?"

"I . . . I don't know. I never try . . . sea-real."

"I like Captain Peanuts best. It's my favorite." Lucy fluffed her pillow and organized the pile of stuffed fake animals next to her head. "Will you get me a bowl? With milk? Mom said it was okay."

"Where?"

"In the kitchen. Go into the pantry next to the sink. And it's the RED BOX!"

I shrugged and walked off to the kitchen. Mrs. Buckworth was playing with her flowers in the backyard, and Mr. Buckworth was in the bathroom singing.

Very lucky. I didn't want to go back to stupid Day Camp. I wanted to stay at the Buckworths' house with Lucy and eat cereal. Rooney and Puddles followed behind me, wagging their tails. I had no idea what a "pan tree" was, but I saw a skinny door next to the sink. I opened the door and stuck my head in. Rooney and Puddles stuck their heads in too.

The room was dark and filled with shelves of cans and boxes. I didn't see any pans or trees. I couldn't even find a light so I could stare at everything. Perfect. If a war suddenly came to America, the pantry was exactly where I would hide. Dark and secret. I'd hide behind red boxes and the soldiers would never find me.

There was so much food that I really couldn't believe it was all for the Buckworths. They were camels. Storing up. Maybe they were saving food for Mayda and Nanny too, and the whole neighborhood. Either way, the Buckworths must've been very afraid that a war was going to come to America. Because nobody, not even George and me, was that hungry.

I could see, sort of, a row of boxes way up high; at least twenty of them in a line on the top shelf. There was a RED BOX in the center. But I think there were a few red boxes—my bad eye was playing tricks—so I wasn't sure which box was which.

I climbed up on the lower shelf and reached my hand up as high as it would go. Not high enough. So I climbed onto the next shelf. My longest finger just barely touched a RED BOX. So I climbed even higher, onto the next shelf, and grabbed on to a heavy can of beans. Wobbly and shaky, I inched the RED BOX out . . .

Rooney and Puddles looked up and drooled.

I almost had the RED BOX in my whole hand, when suddenly the boxes all started to tilt. I tried to stand them straight again, but one of my feet slid, the can of beans crashed to the floor, and suddenly . . . I was falling.

"Helllllp!"

I landed like a lump. Boxes hit my head and flakes of colored puffs fell like snow. All over my hair and my pajamas.

Rooney slobbered and started to eat. Crunch crunch. Puddles had a box in her mouth and was shaking it back and forth. I picked cereal out of my hair and ate a whole bunch of handfuls off the floor. Ick ick yummy.

I liked cereal, but the pantry was a big, crunchy mess.

"EAT, dogs!" I cried. "Faster!" I tried to sweep all the cereal under the bottom shelf with my feet, so the Buckworths wouldn't know that I'd found their hiding place. While the dogs were wildly eating, I grabbed a red box off the floor and went into the kitchen and poured some cereal into a bowl for Lucy. Then I opened the refrigerator and took out some milk. I poured milk to the tippy top of the bowl.

I walked straight to Lucy's room and put her bowl right on her lap.

Lucy's whole face scrunched up in one second. "Ew. Vomit. Why did you give me a bowl of dog food?" I was confused when she hollered, "BETTI! I am NOT a DOG!"

Soon Lucy was going crazy in her pink room. "Will you watch TV with me, Betti? Pleassse?"

I was very scared of the TV, but I sat on Lucy's bed with her because she was broken and it was my fault.

First we watched a "car tooon" where a chicken blew up a rat. There was nothing left of him but a puff of smoke and a tail. While Lucy laughed and laughed, I covered both of my eyes with my hands.

"Betti?" Lucy took her little finger and opened my good eye. "What? What's the matter?"

"It is *not* funny," I said. "It is very, very sad." I stood up immediately because I was going to draw all of this in my Empty Book. Rat tails and chicken cackles and things blowing up.

"Wait!" cried Lucy. "Let's watch a movie then. A funny movie!"

I looked at her big fat foot. I sighed. And sat back down on her bed.

So we watched a movie, even though I was scared at first, because the Melons in the movies had the biggest faces in the world. Sometimes they did some funny things that made Lucy and me laugh like crazy. But most of the time those movie Melons had some serious problems. I sniffled and my eyes got cloudy because I couldn't help it.

"It's not real, Betti. The people aren't real. The rat and the chicken aren't real. Those things aren't really happening. They're just stories. It's just TV."

Big Mouth stories? I wasn't sure about that. Not sure at all. And my stories were definitely better anyway.

Soon Lucy let out a snort like a sleeping cow, and she wasn't even faking. She was sleeping.

Suddenly I had a brilliant idea.

Lucy was trapped in bed. And Mr. Buckworth was walking the dogs. And Mrs. Buckworth was busy doing business and chewing on her pencil, so I couldn't bug her and give her warts, or drive her crazy and make her go wooooooo.

That's when I decided to make my very own circus camp home. Under the tree and next to the swing set. Much better than that ugly pink Melon dollhouse.

I pulled grass out of the ground and cleared a little space. In the center, I made a fire circle out of sticks. I made long paths in the dirt going in two directions. One path led all the way through the woods, past the murky swamp, and down to the village. The other path led down to the river. I had an area for the pig yard, and the pig trough with sloppy slop, and a whole clump of pigs, which were actually little rocks.

I took a shoebox from my closet and took out the fancy shoes. I cut lots of bars all over the box, so the leftover kids and I could see up to the sky. That was my lion cage. I also made a snake tree with a Snake Lady and squiggly snakes out of toothpaste. I stuck big branches from the Buckworths' tree all over the place for my woods. My dolls were little leftover kids made out of sticks, with nuts stuck on top for their heads. Auntie Moo, of course, was the tallest stick of all. Then I thought about things and added a sad little Mrs. Buckworth stick so she would have a home too.

Last of all, I sprinkled my jar of dirt—all the way from the circus camp—over my home.

It wasn't much, it didn't look exactly like the circus camp, but it was the best I could do.

I could practically see Auntie Moo sleeping next to

the fire. I could see the leftover kids napping in the lion cage, crunched into the corner as usual.

At the circus camp I didn't have to show anybody how I walked on my line into the sky. The leftover kids knew I was a star. In my stories I never tripped and never fell.

That was when my Big Mouth stories were very, very important and no one ever laughed.

I could practically hear George's voice before we left for America. "How does it end, Babo? The story? About the beautiful circus girl?" And I answered, "Well, she had to leave. But then she had good luck, and she came back again . . ."

It seemed like a hundred years ago.

I could still watch over my circus camp. Well, at least a little. I could make sure that they were still happy, that there were no soldiers in the woods. I could make sure that nothing was falling from the sky.

I climbed the Buckworths' tallest tree.

I sang back at the red birds on a branch. I watched squirrels chew on nuts and drop them on Rooney's head. I reached my hand up, trying to touch my mama, the tallest woman in the world. And I watched over my circus camp. My mama was watching over the circus camp too. I was sure of it.

"Betti!"

Mr. Buckworth was calling for me inside the house. I

saw Mrs. Buckworth look out the window of my yellow room. I barely heard Lucy say, "Mom, where did she GO?"

The Buckworths never would have found me if it hadn't been for Puddles. Puddles sat at the bottom of the tree and howled and howled until Mr. Buckworth came outside.

"What are you doing up there, little tiger?" Mr. Buckworth tilted his head up and scratched it. His copper coin hair shined in the sun and a few nuts fell next to his feet. "Betti?" he called up into the tree. "How'd you get up there?"

I called down softly, "I am the brave one."

Disaster

AUNTIE MOO TAUGHT me the difference between natural disasters and people disasters. Nature is much more powerful than people. There isn't much anyone can do to stop a natural disaster. But people disasters? Well, Auntie Moo said that those happen when very foolish people make very foolish mistakes.

The Summer Six's disaster was enormous. And it tilted to one side. It looked like a freaky foreign monster had dropped out of the sky and straight onto the play yard of Betsy Ross Elementary School.

Ms. Stacy had shown us a picture of some foreign "volkaynoo" in a book about science. Then she had lined up bowls and spoons, a whole bunch of balloons, a few bags of flour, and a stack of newspapers on a wooden table. She said that we were going to make a much better volcano than the picture in the science book.

So ours grew and grew until it was at least ten times bigger.

I was glad that I got to make a volcano at Day Camp. After two days of sitting home with sprained Lucy, and watching Big Mouth TV stories, I was ready to go back. I'd read Auntie Moo's letter all sorts of times and she said that I had to try very hard in America. I had to teach something and learn something every day. Well, I'd learned enough already. Now, before I ran away, I needed to teach the Summer Five important lessons about my country, and my circus, and me.

After lunch Ms. Stacy said we had to paint the ugly volcano. "Paint your dreams, Summer Six. Maybe it's something you want to be someday . . . a career. It's good to dream big, Summer Six," she said. "The world is your oyster."

I had no idea why Ms. Stacy thought the world was an oyster, but Timmy told Ms. Stacy that he hated oysters. Slimy.

Sam mumbled under her breath, "I hate this artsy flaky learning stuff." She blew an enormous blue bubble that popped in her face and got stuck in her hair.

"What is a car ear?" I whispered to Timmy.

"It's a job," he answered, and wiped his nose on his shirt.

My dream was easy. I dreamed about the circus. It was going to be my Car Ear. Of course.

Then I saw Mayda walking through the play yard of Betsy Ross Elementary. I looked for Nanny too, walking slowly in her slipper shoes, but Mayda was alone. Her back was hunched over and her nose was practically stuffed inside her book. She tripped over something, but she didn't care. She moved her crooked pink glasses up on her nose and looked around at the day campers in circles.

Mayda didn't sit on her regular bench. She timidly sat on the grass, close to the Summer Six, and stared up at the clouds.

It took the Summer Six all afternoon to paint the huge volcano, which wasn't even dry from the morning. It became a mess of bright and dark colors all mixed together with ugly white goo. Definitely not like the volcano in the book.

As I painted, I kept bugging out my bad eye at Bobby Ray to make him really scared.

All of us were completely quiet when Ms. Stacy asked us each to say something about our paintings.

"Well, my dream is to be an ambulance driver," Timmy started, pointing at a painted heart with a happy face on the volcano. "I am thankful because the ambulance driver saved my grandpa when his heart had an attack."

"Who attacked it? Aliens?" hooted Jerry.

"No," answered Timmy. "I don't know why it got attacked."

Bobby Ray painted a fish on a hook. He wanted to be a fisherman because he liked sitting in a boat all day and drinking Coke. The fish's eyes stared off like it was looking at something very important somewhere else. It is very sad to be a fish.

Tabitha painted a big blob with glasses. She dreamed of being a lawyer so she could be really tough like the people on TV, and Jerry wanted to be a big oval ball. He dreamed of being a football player, he said, which is probably why he painted a ball that looked like a big fat foot.

When it was Sam's turn she announced, "I would like to be a rock singer. In a rock band."

"You?" said Jerry. Bobby Ray and he burst out laughing.

Sam had painted a picture of a tall person with tall spiky purple hair and colorful clothes. "I have a song," Sam told us, "that I wrote myself." She cleared her throat and suddenly . . . started to sing. I didn't understand why anyone would want to be a rock, but Sam's singing was very screechy.

Then it was my turn because I was the only one left. I was all ready to teach the Summer Five important lessons about my country and me, but I was sweating and my hands were shaking.

"I paint pictures," I said softly, "of my . . . car ear."

I pointed to the very top of the volcano.

Sam stopped chewing her gum long enough to ask: "What *is* it?"

Timmy squinted. "Is it a dog?"

"It is . . . a very tall fork. I mean, woman. In the world. With tail," I squeaked. I had also painted a purple elephant, and a lion wearing roller skates, and a snake lady holding all sorts of lucky squiggly snakes.

"Weird," said Bobby Ray.

"Betti, do you want to work at the zoo?" asked Ms. Stacy, looking awfully confused.

"No," I started slowly. I had also painted a soldier who probably looked like a zoo man, but I didn't want Ms. Stacy to put me in the zoo. "I want to be in the circus. Again. I *was* in the circus. Before. Before it burned."

The Summer Five stared.

So out of nowhere I added: "And that is where my eye got broken." I pointed at my fish eye.

Timmy gulped. "In the circus? How?"

"What happened?" gasped Tabitha with her mouth wide open.

Suddenly, I was *very* interesting. My words tumbled out in a mish-mash of gobbledygook. "Well . . . I walk on a . . . a line . . . up in the sky."

"The high wire?" asked Timmy, spitting out of his wire teeth and squinting his eyes.

"Yes. High Wire." I didn't know what a high wire was, but I was sure I must've walked on it. I went on: "My mama stands at one end of high wire. She is the tallest woman. In a whole world. With a tail."

"WHAT?" hooted Jerry. "No way."

"And my dad . . . he is green." I didn't know the words for bumpy or alligator so I sort of pinched at my body. "He stands down at bottom." I pointed at the ground. "To catch me. If I fall."

"Totally freaky," exclaimed Bobby Ray.

"The people watch me. They pay banana. And they go like this." I clapped for effect. "But one night Snake Lady, named Sister Baroo, falls asleep. Her snakes ran away. And one of her snakes crawled up . . . up into the sky . . . on my high wire.

"The snake"—I puffed up my chest, my arms rose up—"its head came to my face, like this. SSSSSSS." I hissed at the Summer Five and they all scooted back on the grass. "Sister Baroo say, 'That snake is magic! It will give you good luck. Or bad luck. It is hard to say.' And then . . . the snake takes tongue . . ." I stuck out my tongue and wagged it around for effect. ". . . and eats my eye."

"Gross." Tabitha looked like she was going to be sick.

"Boy," said Ms. Stacy. "Wow."

"My eye is broken." I shook my head sadly and bugged out my bad eye.

"Sounds like bad luck to me," mumbled Bobby Ray.

I shrugged. "But people love me. 'We love you,' they say. And they love my bad eye."

"Where are they then?" asked Sam, scratching at her hair. "That Sister Baroo snake lady? And your mom and dad?"

I took a deep breath. "They are lost. Maybe mermaids. They sing. With ghosts. And they look . . . for me. But I am not a toast. I mean, a ghost."

Bobby Ray had a little smile on his face. "That seriously doesn't make any sense."

And that's when the mean boys started laughing like crazy.

I looked around for George in the clusters of campers. He was far across the play yard making sand blobs. He kept looking up to watch the second graders climb the enormous funny-colored things coming out of the ground. They were swinging like monkeys with their arms. Even though George couldn't swing because of his lost arm, he didn't care. I could hear him giggling as if it was the best day of his life. Which just figured.

I looked over at Mayda too. She'd been listening very carefully to my story, I could tell. Her nose was out of her book and her eyes were wide open, watching everything.

After Ms. Stacy hushed up the mean boys, Timmy

asked, "When do we get to make lava come out of the volcano, Ms. Stacy?"

"Right now, Timmy. I'll be right back, kids. Sit quietly please." Ms. Stacy ran off to get lava supplies.

I had no idea what lava was, but I definitely wanted to see it.

Suddenly out of stupid Bobby Ray's mouth came, "I'm a starrrr. In the circussss."

I moved my lips but no words came out.

"And that's where I broke my eye!" Jerry pretended to poke his finger in his eye. He fell over backward and rolled around on the grass. "The snakes! They ATE it!"

I pretended that my ears were out of order.

"It's a good thing my mama and dad are coming any day . . ."

And then I'd had it.

"They ARE coming to get me!" I shouted as loud as I could. I gave Bobby Ray and Jerry the meanest scariest look my bad eye could give. "I AM IN THE CIRCUS! You do not understand ANYTHING."

Suddenly . . . our huge volcano exploded! My Big Mouth made our balloons pop one by one, which made our volcano cave into one big pile of crusty mush.

"Whoa," said Tabitha.

"Seriously freaky," said Bobby Ray.

"Ew," said Timmy.

"Oh my goodness," said Ms. Stacy, who'd come jogging back when she heard me screaming. She slapped her hand to her forehead.

Sam took the wad of gum out of her mouth and stuck it on the mess of goo.

"I hate this art project flaky stuff," she said, picking globs of white volcano out of her pointy hair.

I looked over and saw Mayda laughing on the grass, at least a little. So I laughed a little too.

Our volcano lay in a huge flat, floury, popped balloon-ey heap all over the wooden table. Maybe this was the lava. No one had anything to say—no Big Mouth words—as we all stared at it. I thought it'd probably be stuck there forever. At least maybe the Summer Five learned one thing from my important lessons:

This was definitely a people disaster.

Little Traitor and My Trip

I STOMPED ACROSS the play yard in a straight line. I was practicing for the circus. I was going to practice all night. Those mean boys didn't know anything.

"Babo! Babo!"

Even in America George was about the slowest runner in the whole world. His new backpack bounced up and down like a sack of potatoes.

"You want . . . swimming poo?" George tilted his head and his eyes stared into space. He was trying to think of the right words. "Play with we? My horse. For KOOKEY. And swim?"

My feet teetered. "I do not want a swimming poo or a horse, George. And I cannot play with you because I have to think about my car ear." I rubbed my watery eyes dry.

George ducked his head as a ball flew through the air and nearly took off his big ear. "Car ear? What is car ear?" He put his finger on my wet cheek. "What's the matter, Babo?"

"America is horrible. Stupid. Crazy." I put my nose in the air and held my arms out. My hands were curled as pretty as possible. "I want to go home. To—"

"To our circus camp," George said softly. "I know, Babo. You always do."

"I've thought and thought about it. I've tried to be bad and the Buckworths still love me. So I've decided that we have to run away. Any day now. We have to try to run back to the big bird plane, and back to Big Uncle's taxi, and back home."

George was quiet. Finally he said, "But . . . I already have a home, Babo. I don't want to go back there." He looked back at the play yard. "I like it here."

I stepped off my high wire line. I put my arm around George and made him sit down next to me on the grass. "What about the circus? When it comes back again?"

George poked his finger into the dirt. "I don't think I can be in the circus anyway."

I knew he was thinking about his lost arm. "Everyone in the circus is broken, George."

"I want to be a doctor for animals. My mommy said I could be a doctor for animals someday."

"Our circus *needs* a doctor for animals. It's a very important job, George. Think about it."

He thought about it. "But—"

"I can't leave you here all by yourself. *Alone*. In crazy America! You might get lost."

George tapped his finger on my knee and looked up at me. "My mommy won't let me get lost. And I'm not alone. I have my mommy, and some new friends, and I have you, but—"

"Don't you see? You're forgetting your real family. The leftover kids. You're forgetting everything." I stood up and stomped my foot. "Just like a traitor."

Traitor was a bad, bad word in my country. George's bottom lip stuck out like he was about to cry.

Then I started walking fast, really fast, on my invisible high wire line, which had become crooked. George tried to catch up with me, knocking into my heels.

"No, Babo! I never forget them!"

I started counting my perfect steps—twenty-four, twenty-five, twenty-six—when I heard George's mommy calling for him. Suddenly George wasn't following me anymore. He was standing on the sidewalk, stuck.

"I must go, Babo. My mommy—"

"I know."

"Babo, to-morr-ow? Swimming poo? My horse house?"

"Tomorrow," I hollered back at him, "I may be gone."

"I don't want you to go, Babo!" George called out to me and sniffled like crazy. "I want you to be happy. With me. Here!"

I didn't answer. But I did turn around and watch George. His mommy was waiting for him across the play yard. His second-grade Melon friend, named Stephanie, was waiting too. She was probably going to get a cookie, and swim in his swimming pool. George used to ask me every day at the circus camp if he could be *my* best friend. Now he ran toward his new mommy and his new friend.

And then he was gone.

Forty-eight. Step step step. Fifty-one. Step step. Fifty-three. I was definitely going to be a circus star. This was just the beginning. I'd be so good that the circus people would *never* leave me behind. They'd need me. I'd be so good that everyone would clap for me, even the Summer Five.

I was watching my feet so closely, staring at my bright white play shoes, that I almost tripped over a book on the grass. A few books actually. And Mayda. Her legs were crossed on a curb between the grass and the street.

"Hi Babo Betti," said Mayda. "Are you going home now?" Her face was all red and patchy. From a terrible rash, or from picking, or from crying, it was hard to say.

"Um, yes?"

"Do you want to walk with me?" Mayda looked a

little nervous as she picked up her books in her arms, and dropped two back on the ground. "I think we go the same way."

"I . . . I have to wait," I answered. "For Mrs. Buckworth."

Mayda looked down and tapped her dirty shoe against the cement.

"But . . . you can wait too," I suddenly blurted out. "And walk with me too. And Mrs. Buckworth too."

Mayda looked up and smiled. "Okay!"

So I sat down next to Mayda and we waited. We kicked our heels against the curb.

She finally asked, "Were you really in a circus, Betti?"

I nodded. And gulped.

"That's really cool."

"Yes. It was . . . is . . . cool." Which must've been the word for when the wind blew in my face when I was on the high wire.

"Is it a traveling circus?"

"Um, we have home . . . a camp . . . but we travel. All over the world."

"I travel too." Mayda bit her chapped lip. "It's not nearly so cool as being in a circus though."

"What is your car ear dream?" I asked her.

"Me? Oh, well, I guess I want to be a photographer. I don't know if it'll happen though."

I had no idea what a photographer was, but I told her, "The world is an oyster."

Mayda just shrugged.

I wanted to ask Mayda where she had come from and why she was a new student, and why she wasn't in Day Camp like everybody else, and why Nanny lived next door sometimes. But Mayda didn't look like she wanted to talk about any of it. Her lips were locked. Ugh.

Instead she said, "Do you think you can show me? I mean, what you did? On your high wire?"

"I don't know. I . . ." I squeaked. "I . . . I need a line . . . up to . . . the sky."

But Mayda's eyes sparkled behind her pink glasses as she looked up at the clouds. "It doesn't have to be in the sky, Betti. It can be right here."

So I couldn't say no. My knees were shaking as I stood up. "I . . . I walk like . . . this." I put my arms out. I took one step. And another step. I curled my pinky fingers as if I was a real star. I raised my head in the air like an exotic bird, and tried to point my missing toes. One graceful step and another.

And then . . .

I tripped on a clump of grass. "Ow ow," I slurred. "Ow."

Mayda gasped. "Are you okay?"

I nodded and rubbed my bad eye like I had a bug in it. Very clumsy.

"That was still pretty good," said Mayda. "I bet you're really good."

I smiled, just a little, because I couldn't help it.

When Mrs. Buckworth came to pick up Mayda and me a few minutes later, we walked quietly past the old bicycle in the yard and the skateboard. Past the garden and the pond and the quacking ducks. Past the mailbox and the tree house. And then, after we reached Mayda's house, Mayda turned to me and asked, "I wondered if, maybe, you would like to come back to my house? I mean, to play? Would you like to play with me someday soon?"

Mayda didn't understand that I couldn't have any friends in America. I was going to be running away any day, and I had a terrible time leaving friends. But Mayda's face looked awfully hopeful.

Finally I stammered, "O . . . okay," because she was probably broken.

"Really?" Mayda's face lit up. "That'd be great!" She smiled as if I'd just given her a big fat present.

Invasion of My Circus Camp

SOMETHING WAS VERY, very wrong.

Malibu Margie and Ramon had squished my snake tree and knocked over some leftover kids. Roller Derby Tina was sitting right in the middle of my fire circle. Jessie Lynn was smiling in her wedding dress on top of my lion cage.

"I just want to play with it!" cried Lucy as I tossed her dolls one by one over my shoulder into the grass. "Please?" Her foot was still enormous but she was walking around with wooden sticks under her arms. "WHY can't I, Betti?"

"Your dolls are too . . . perfect." I watched an ant crawl through my miniature fire circle. "Circus people are not perfect."

"My dolls aren't that perfect." Lucy held Roller Derby

Tina up to her nose. Tina's head was a bit squished from the roller skate accident.

"And . . ." I put my nose in the air. "It is MY home. For circus people."

"What circus? I don't see any circus people!" Lucy picked up all of her plastic people and waved them over my circus camp. They were three times bigger than the Hairy Bear Boy's empty tent or the snake tree.

"You can't see them." I carefully fixed the lion cage and propped up the trees. "Because you don't have a special eye. Like me."

"Maybe I can see them too. I'll look really hard." Lucy's eyes got all squinty and googley as she stared at the ground. "I'm pretty sure I see them now. Yeah, I do. My dolls will just practice here. On these rocks."

"Those are NOT rocks. You are smooshing my pigs!"

"Well." Lucy rubbed her eyes. Her bottom lip stuck out like she was going to cry. "They don't look like pigs to me. And the rest of it doesn't look like a circus. It looks like a bunch of sticks." Lucy gathered her dolls in a clump and stood up. "I'm going to make my own circus then. In my dollhouse. And everyone will come and see it." She tried to carry her dolls as she hobbled on her wooden sticks toward the house. "You may not even be invited, Betti."

I shrugged. I moved my pig rocks into a circle. A chorus of rock-singing pigs. The tall Auntie Moo stick and the Babo stick—me—sat next to the river washing our clothes, and laughing private laughs.

In about one second Lucy was back. "Can't I play with yours? Yours is better."

I sighed and carefully put my sticks down. "You must be born in the circus. Not in America."

"How come you're so bossy?" cried Lucy. "You weren't born in any ol' circus!"

"Yes." I took a deep dramatic breath so I could begin my Big Mouth story. "In my circus, Fifi the elephant did show and clowns with red hair stood on her back."

"Did the clowns have hair like my hair?"

I nodded. "And Teeny-Tiny Puppet Man did funny show about war."

Lucy squatted down next to me in the dirt. Her fat foot knocked down the Teeny-Tiny Puppet Man as she put her little hands on my feet.

"One day . . . soldiers come to circus camp. Fifi the elephant scream, 'Climb up, climb up on me!' She put her big fat nose in the air. So Teeny-Tiny Puppet Man climbed up on the clowns, and the Hairy Bear Boy climbed on Teeny-Tiny Puppet Man, and Cindi the lion—"

Lucy scrunched her eyes. "The lion climbed on top of the elephant?"

"BOOM!" I continued, and Lucy scooted back in the grass.

"What was the boom?"

"A bomb."

"A bomb?"

"And Big Uncle's tire. Boom!" I wildly waved my arms around for effect. "He climb up too. And Auntie Moo. And the leftover kids. I climb on very top. My dad wait below to catch us if we fall. But . . . we did not fall."

Lucy's eyes were wide open. She was listening very carefully, so I went on.

"My mama waits for us. She is tallest woman in the world. She lifts us into the sky. In her hands. Big, big hands. Over the trees, over the high wire." I raised my hands and stared dramatically into the Buckworths' big tree.

Lucy looked confused. "My mom said that your mom and dad *died*, Betti. A long time ago."

My whole body suddenly got stiffer than a scarecrow in a bean field. Birds could've made nests on my head and I wouldn't have noticed.

Lucy had a very Big Mouth. But my Big Mouth was louder.

"NO!" I practically shouted, jumping up from the grass. "We are lucky. Mama and Dad and all circus people. We are IN THE SKY."

Fluffing up Jessie Lynn's wedding dress, Lucy said, "Well, my mom said that your parents weren't saved. And that's why you got to come live here, Betti." She tilted her head and looked up at me. "That's why we wanted you to be in *our* family 'Cause you were an orphan."

My good eye was watering so much that I had to rub it, as if I was shooing away a hundred bugs. My nose was running so much that I had to wipe it with my sleeve. "No! We are SAFE."

Lucy shrugged. "That's not what Mom said."

I had to practice for the circus. Immediately. I had to walk on my high wire line.

Mrs. Buckworth had a long green snake line that she used to water her flowers. Perfect. I stepped onto it gracefully and walked on perfect toes across the middle of the yard. My pinky fingers were curled up and my toes were pointed. I didn't see anything but my high wire.

"Can't I be in your circus, Betti?"

Step step step. One foot at a time.

"Please?"

Step step. I couldn't hear a single word.

"Sometimes you're not nice, Betti."

I needed to hear the circus music. I needed to keep walking.

But suddenly . . . water was flying everywhere! It hit me and just about everything else like a monsoon. Lucy had the other end of the green snake and was whipping it around in her little hands.

My whole head was drenched. Water dripped off my lashes and into my eyes as I slid right off my line and into the mushy grass.

"I'm giving a bath to the circus animals!" Lucy hollered. Rooney and Puddles shook water off and hid under Mrs. Buckworth's bushes.

My stick trees were buried and my leftover stick people were soggy. My fire circle was a little swimming pool.

That's when my Big Mouth came back with a roar. "Your dolls are SOLDIERS! Do you not see? They are Melons! Too big. They stomp my people. My people disappear. They wash away!"

Lucy's eyes grew huge. Scared. In a tiny peep she said, "My dolls aren't going to hurt anybody, Betti. My dolls are nice dolls. We just want to play."

"NO!" I shouted. "Tricky!"

Lucy's whimpers turned into loud jaggedy sobs. "Well I—hate you—sometimes!" She stood up and stomped her good foot and shouted, "'Cause you're mean. Really really MEAN!"

I put my hands over my ears. I searched for the Auntie Moo stick by the river. I searched for Babo.

Suddenly Mrs. Buckworth was standing outside. "LUCY!"

But it didn't matter anyway.

I ran like I was running from the soldiers. Straight

past Mrs. Buckworth to the pantry. I crawled under the shelves of boxes and cans and made myself as small as I could, almost invisible, into a tiny ball.

I heard Lucy bawling and I heard Mrs. Buckworth saying, "Did you say something, Lucy? What did you say to Betti?"

"Nothing! Well, I said she was MEAN."

"You need to say you're sorry."

"NO! She *is* mean. I don't want a big sister!"

I wanted to stay in my hiding place pantry forever. No one would ever find me. Of course, the Buckworths didn't want to find me anyway. I was sure of it. I wasn't even their real kid. And I was a mean and horrible big sister too. Finally the Buckworths definitely realized that they'd made the wrong choice. Finally they understood everything.

But when Mr. Buckworth found me hiding in the pantry and picked me up in his big bear arms, I didn't even have the energy to fight like a little tiger. When Mrs. Buckworth smoothed my hair and Mr. Buckworth carried me into my yellow room, I didn't have the energy to explain to them—again—how very horrible I was.

It was all so confusing.

"My heart. It has been attacked." I dramatically put my hand right over my sore heart.

Mr. Buckworth chuckled, just a little. "You're probably not having a heart attack, little tiger. You're probably just missing people—missing *everything*—in your country. That's normal. But sometimes that's even worse."

I pulled my circus doll off my pillow and sat her in my lap. "I . . . do not want you to get mad," I blurted out without meaning to.

Mrs. Buckworth crinkled her forehead. "Why would we be mad?"

"Sometimes I think . . . my mama and dad . . . I think they will come and get me in America. Here. At your house. But then . . . I am sometimes afraid they will not come." I looked at Mrs. Buckworth. "Like your mama and dad."

Mr. and Mrs. Buckworth glanced at each other.

"Betti." Mr. Buckworth cleared his throat. "Auntie Moo told us how the soldiers came to the camp a long time ago, and the circus people tried to fight back. They stood up for themselves; they fought for what they believed in, but they didn't have guns. They only had their animals, right?"

I nodded.

Mrs. Buckworth's eyes became a little wet. "Auntie Moo said that your mom and dad, and all the circus people, didn't have a fair chance."

"No," I choked out. "It was not fair."

"But they saved *you*, sweetie. The most loving thing

parents can ever do. They hid you away when the soldiers came. They must've loved you so much."

I hugged my doll against my chest.

"And now," said Mr. Buckworth, "they'd be so proud of you, Betti. You're brave, like them. You stand up for yourself like a little tiger."

"My mama is the Tallest Woman in the World. With a Tail." I looked up at the yellow ceiling, but I couldn't see my mama. "And my dad is green man. If they come to your door you will know." I looked at the fuzzy floor. No green dad with his arms ready to catch me. "If the leftover kids or Auntie Moo come to your door, you will know."

The Buckworths both put their arms around me in one big tight hug.

"They're my family too." My voice was all sniffley and muffled. "You won't be mad if I have two families?"

"No, little tiger. We just feel lucky," said Mr. Buckworth, "to be your second family."

"Some people don't have any family," said Mrs. Buckworth, who didn't used to have a family, "but you have two."

Just like I had two names. Babo and Betti.

Even though the Buckworths could be very crazy at times, it wasn't all that bad being squished between them.

But I wasn't squished for long, because that's when

the Buckworths noticed something funny. Rooney. And Puddles. They'd jumped off my bed and were sneakily chomping on things in my secret room closet.

Mr. and Mrs. Buckworth curiously walked over there too. They both leaned down to look inside my orange bag.

"Oh!" Mrs. Buckworth slapped her hand over her mouth.

Mr. Buckworth itched his head. "What the—"

They didn't know the right words to say even though they spoke English.

I had saved a whole lot. Leftovers. Cookies and apples and cereal and toast and pizza and weird boxes of juice. It was all still there, stored up, because I hadn't been starving yet. I hadn't starved a single day at the Buckworths'. I wasn't even really a skin-'n'-bones chicken.

That's when I barely whispered, "I am a camel," even though it didn't mean much anymore.

THAT NIGHT WHEN I was in my bed, a bright circle of light shined on me. I rubbed my eye. A bad dream? A sweet dream?

It was a flashlight. "We're having a slumber party, Betti!" Lucy whispered way too loud. "Shhhhh." She dropped her dolls in a heap by my head and trailed her spotlight over her dolls. "Betti, look at my dolls! Aren't they . . . BEAUTIFUL?"

Roller Derby Tina had a tail and one of her feet looked huge, just like Lucy's. There was cloth wrapped around her roller skate. Malibu Margie was covered in black fur, which looked suspiciously like Rooney's fur. Ramon had crayon all over his face like a scary clown. Jimmy Dale's overalls were green and lumpy, and Jessie Lynn, still in her wedding dress, had an enormous blown-up head. Probably from the microwave.

Lucy crawled into my bed and laid her head on my potato sack. I almost felt the way I used to feel in the lion cage. With the leftover kids crunched up next to me so they wouldn't have nightmares.

"Betti? I'm sorry. About your mom and dad. But I'm happy you get to be my sister. Do you think I can be in your circus too? Can I? I mean, if my dolls aren't perfect? And I'm not perfect?"

I thought about things. "Yes," I finally whispered back. "You can be in my circus."

Lucy fell asleep about one second later with her ponytail touching my cheek. I moved my feet right up against her cold little feet. And my feet stayed there, just like that.

My Leftover Friend

THE NEXT DAY Mrs. Buckworth said that I could play at
Mayda's house. Even if Lenore, the adoption expert lady,
said that I'd adapt if I made some friends and learned
some English—and I definitely wasn't going to adapt—
I'd promised to play with Mayda, my English teacher,
someday soon. And my promises were always good.

So Mrs. Buckworth called Mayda's mama, and I
guess she said it'd be just marvelous if I came over and
played. When Mrs. Buckworth dropped me off, Mayda
told Mrs. Buckworth that her dad was home but he was
taking a bath at that exact moment.

"But we'll bring Betti home this afternoon, okay? By
three?" Mayda smiled politely at Mrs. Buckworth. Her
teeth were a little crooked, just like all the leftover kids'
teeth.

Mrs. Buckworth nodded. "Well, I guess it's . . . okay. But will you call if you need anything, girls? Please?" Mrs. Buckworth looked a little worried, again. "And have lots of fun."

We said good-bye to Mrs. Buckworth and I followed Mayda inside. As soon as she shut her front door, she turned to me and said, "You probably shouldn't tell your mom that we're here alone."

"You live all by yourself? In your house?"

"Kind of," she answered mysteriously. "Well, my dad lives here too, but it's mostly me."

If I lived all by myself in Mayda's house, I would definitely adopt all the leftover kids and Auntie Moo.

"See, I know my mom's voice perfectly." Mayda pulled out a bag of bread in her kitchen. "I just acted like her on the phone because I wanted you to come play with me." She started slathering brown nutty goo on the bread. "I'm making us a little snack. Peanut butter sandwiches. I hope you're hungry."

I was always hungry. "But, where is you mama then?" My eyes darted around Mayda's empty skeleton living room.

"My mom? Oh, she lives in New Jersey. She calls me, though. On my birthday."

I nodded. It was all very confusing.

"So I live with my dad. But he works a lot. Basically he has to work all the time. Two jobs. But it's okay." Mayda laid pieces of chocolate candy on top of our peanut bread. "I don't want people to think that he's a bad dad. He's a really good dad. He wants to be here with me all the time, but I tell him I'm fine by myself. I get to be with Nanny too. And when my dad comes home at night we tell each other all the funny stories about our day."

Mayda pulled white, squishy things out of a plastic bag and smooshed them on top of the chocolate candy. "I hope you like marshmallows." Mayda stuffed a whole one in her mouth and handed me one, so I stuffed it in my mouth. Fluffy. "I love marshmallows," she said, squashing more of them on top of the chocolate.

"Ick," I replied. "Mayda, you do not want to go to Day Camp?"

"Oh, we can't really afford it. We're broke."

I stared at her blankly. "You are broken?"

"No, we . . . don't have enough money."

I understood the word "money," and I was pretty sure that Mayda didn't have any.

"My dad is saving money for me to go to college. Just a little at a time. He says I'm too smart not to go to college." Mayda finally finished by plopping two pieces of bread on top of her two chocolate-marshmallow-peanut butter towers. She handed one to me. "Anyway," continued Mayda, taking a big bite out of her sandwich, "some of those kids can be mean and horrible. I'd probably hate Day Camp."

I thought about the mean and nasty dudes at Day Camp. I looked out of the corner of my good eye at Mayda. "Have they been . . . horrible to you too?"

"Oh sure. Not these kids, but other kids. You know, at other schools. Ugh."

I nodded. Ugh. We both had the locked lip sickness about nasty dudes.

"But it doesn't matter. I don't care if kids laugh at me. They never really get to know me." Mayda shrugged. "We just move a lot."

"You and Nanny?"

"No. My dad and me. Sometimes it's hard to find jobs. Sometimes we think it'll be easier in a different place. But it's never really that much easier. Right now my dad has two jobs, so that's good. He cleans buildings."

"Buildings in the sky?"

Mayda smiled and nodded. "He may get to clean at Betsy Ross too. When school starts."

Mayda motioned for me to follow her into the living room. We sat down on the stained carpet with our sandwiches. She grabbed the little plastic blue dog that was sitting against the wall. "This is the only pet I can have right now 'cause we keep moving."

Mayda pushed a button and the blue barking dog crawled on jerky legs across Mayda's living room floor. It would stop every few steps and bark with plastic teeth. Woof woof woof. I liked Rooney and Puddles better.

"So Nanny is your . . . Grand Mama?" I asked.

"Nanny? No. She's not really my Nanny. I just met her when I moved here at the beginning of summer. She's my friend. She watches out for me and I watch out for her. Today she's sick, though." Mayda looked off into space at nothing. "She's at the doctor. She tells me not to worry."

Almost everyone I knew was sick and I always worried too.

Our mouths were chewing in slow motion, our lips were practically stuck. I was starting to like American food. I definitely was.

"Hey!" Mayda suddenly cried out. "Can I take your picture?"

Before I could answer, Mayda ran down her hall. She came back in about one second and held out a little black box. "This is a camera, see? Nanny gave it to me. I think it's about a hundred years old."

I thought of the pictures I had of the Buckworths in my orange bag. I thought of the picture of Lucy on roller skates, and George's mommy in front of the swimming pool. Now I'd have a picture of ME to send to Auntie Moo.

Mayda stood back and put the camera to her eye and aimed it at me. "Smile, Betti."

But I wasn't used to smiling at a black box so I just squinted as the camera went FLASH and my good eye saw stars.

"Thanks." Mayda set her camera down. "Do you want another sandwich, Betti?"

I didn't know what sand and a witch had to do with bread and marshmallows, but I nodded and said "yummy" anyway. The barking blue dog crashed into the wall and fell over. Its little blue legs waved in the air.

"You can eat it on the way, okay?"

"THERE'S JUST NOT much to do at my house!" Mayda shouted over her shoulder. "It's more fun to go places!"

"I think so too!" I shouted back.

I rode on the back of Mayda's beat-up brown bicycle. We both wore hard hats on our heads, which Mayda called "helmets." My orange bag bounced up and down on my back as we rode over bumps and holes. The cool wind blew in my face and my hair blew out of my helmet. My chocolate marshmallow bread almost flew away, so I stuffed it all in my mouth.

When we arrived at an old building, Mayda left her bike outside leaning against the wall. "No one ever steals this ol' thing," she said. She took off her helmet and swung it around with her hand. "This is the library.

It's one of my favorite places. They let you read books for free. Sometimes I come here with Nanny, and sometimes just by myself."

"The Lie berry," I repeated. "Free books."

The library was very quiet. Probably there were a lot of reading ghosts flying around. "Hi Mayda," said two library ladies when we walked in. Mayda knew everybody at the library. She led me past walls and walls and walls of books. She stopped in the section that said "Children."

"You can choose some, Betti."

"Which one?" I asked, looking at hundreds and thousands of books.

"Any one you want. That's what's cool about the library."

So I closed my good eye and picked one off the shelf. It was enormous and didn't have many words inside, but it had very shiny, funny pictures. Then Mayda picked a book for me. "This is a good one, Betti!" On the front of my new book was a picture of a little piglet and a grandma spider.

"Chair-lett Weeb?"

"Charlotte's Web," said Mayda. "I really like this one!"

I didn't know if I liked my new book or not. But I liked holding it in my hands. I liked touching the pig's pink snout and tracing my finger around the spider's web.

"We'll start easy at first," Mayda said over her shoulder, "and then we'll read harder ones, okay?" She led me past more walls of books to some plastic chairs in a corner. On the way, Mayda stopped in the section that said "Young Adult Fiction" and picked a book off the shelf for herself. Mayda acted like a wise old woman, as if she were already in the ninth grade.

I immediately liked my story of the happy pig and the wise old lady spider. I couldn't understand all of it, but Mayda helped me. When there were words I didn't know, Mayda explained them and I wrote them in my Empty Book so I would remember. Someday, I thought, I would tell this happy pig story to the leftover kids.

That's when Mayda said, "Let's sit by the fountain."

"Okay. Fow Tin." It was like a swimming pool that magically spouted water into the sky. Mayda and I swung our legs back and forth. Then I dunked my arm all the way to the bottom of the water and fished out two coins, which Mayda thought was very funny. One coin for Mayda and one for me.

"Make a wish, Betti," she told me, and closed her eyes. I closed my good eye too.

Finally Mayda said, "I wish my mom would call me. Not just on my birthday." She threw her coin into the water and watched it sink. "I wish she would send me letters. Or postcards even. Or more pictures. Or something."

We were quiet. I was thinking about Mayda's mama, somewhere far, far away, in a New Germ Sea.

"My mom used to take a lot of pictures." Mayda stared straight ahead. "Of my dad and me. I have pictures of all three of us from a long time ago."

"From kamra?"

"Yeah. My dad says that she didn't know what she wanted back then." Mayda shrugged. "She was really young. She just wanted to take pictures—see the world and all that—and not be stuck with a baby. So she ran away basically." Mayda looked down at the book she got from the library, and flipped through some pages without reading them. "But now . . . she has a new family. I guess she forgot about me." She pushed her crooked pink glasses up on her nose and said, "Do you think your parents forgot about you too, Betti?"

Before I could stop myself, I blurted out, "I think . . . my mama and dad . . ." I sucked in my breath. "Died. In the war." I almost melted into the fountain. I couldn't believe the words came out of my Big Mouth.

"Oh." Mayda stopped swinging her legs. "Sorry, Betti."

"They did not run away. They did not forget me," I said. "They save me."

"Do you remember them? At all?"

"No." I shook my head, just a little. "I . . . I do not remember them."

"I barely remember my mom either," said Mayda. "Just pictures. And her voice." Mayda thought about things. "I guess you're lucky, Betti. Well, at least now you have a new mom. And a dad. And they seem so nice."

I was quiet for a long time until I practically whispered, "Yes. I am lucky."

Mayda played with her knotty hair and looked into the water. I think we both understood that neither of us wanted to talk about horrible kids, or moving, or starting school, or about our mamas and dads.

I closed my eyes and wished that Mayda would get another postcard, even though I didn't know what a postcard was. I tossed my coin; it skipped on the blue water and sunk to the bottom.

As we rode away from the library, I clutched my new book and thought about Mayda's mama running away. And sad Mayda.

I climbed off the bicycle at the Buckworths' house and said, "Thank you, Mayda. For being teacher. And playing."

"I had fun, Betti." Mayda smiled and straightened her helmet.

And I thought: This is bad. I was planning to run away too, like Mayda's mama. But I didn't know that running away would make other people—the people who were left behind—so very, very sad.

I was walking to the Buckworths' front door when I heard, "Hey, Betti? You don't have to tell me stories. I mean, you can tell me things that really happened there. In your country. I won't freak out or have nightmares or anything."

Mayda zoomed away on her brown beat-up bicycle.

MY EMPTY BOOK
(Day TWELVE in America)

Sea-real = Captain Peanuts. Crunchy, but not dog food.

Pan tree = Hiding Place.

Car tooon = Not a car. Rat gets blown up.

Moveee on T. = Big faces with Big Mouth stories.

Volkaynoo = A people disaster.

World is your oyster = Car Ear, slimy

Car Ear = Job

Rock Singer = Not a rock. Screechy singing.

Lava = A big gooey disaster.

Coool = High-wire winds.

Photograffer = Mayda's dream car ear.

Blind as a bat = Bats are blind on boats.

Marsh Mellow = Fluffy, squishy on bread.

Kamra = For pictures of me. To send to Auntie Moo.

Sand Witch = Bread with all sorts of stuff inside.
   No sand and no witch.
Helmet = Hard hat for head.
Lie Berry = Thousands of free books.
Post Card = What Mayda wants from her mom.
Fow Tin = Water and wishes.
Orphan = Me, after my mama and dad died.

Frankenstein and the Jungle Wars

I WAS WEARING my circus dress. The raggedy sleeves hung down past my fingers and the jaggedy fringe hung down past my knobby knees. I knew that the few leftover sequins on my dress glittered like water in a fountain.

I was wearing my red buckle special occasion shoes, because this was a special occasion.

My mama and dad would be very proud of me.

I am brave. I am a little tiger. I can sing songs from the circus and not be afraid. I cannot worry if dudes laugh.

"Are you sure you want to go to Day Camp, Betti?" asked Mrs. Buckworth in her worried voice. "You don't have to, you know."

Yes. I wanted to.

I didn't even gobble all of my eggs or my jelly toast at breakfast. Lucy and Mrs. Buckworth fell behind me on the sidewalk as I stomped to Day Camp with my head high in the air.

The Summer Six had free time to play while Ms. Stacy set up supplies for our next "fun activiteee" on the volcano table.

I looked for Mayda and Nanny on their special bench. They weren't there. But I sat there anyway, all by myself. I pulled my Empty Book out of my orange bag so I could read my letter again from Auntie Moo.

I wasn't even sitting for a minute when a ball landed right between my feet.

"Hey circus girl! Nice dress."

Bobby Ray was towering over me like a nasty giant. I stuffed my nose inside my book. He tapped his foot on the ground as I set my red buckle shoes right on top of his ball.

Jerry ran up and socked Bobby Ray in the arm. "Dude, it's your kick."

I took a big breath and touched the picture of my green, bumpy dad.

"Are you gonna give us our ball, or what?"

"Babo! Babo!"

George.

The whole trail of second graders was behind him, skipping and jumping over patches of grass. "Do you want to monkey . . . with we, Babo?" George asked, out of breath.

"*Play*, George. Play with *us*. That's what you say," giggled Stephanie. "By the *monkey bars*." She was George's English teacher, along with Lenore, the adoption expert lady.

"*Us* we . . . monkey playing!" squealed George.

"I cannot be a monkey now, George," I told him.

George smiled and looked down at my Empty Book. He touched my dad picture with his finger. "That is . . . pretty, Babo!"

"It's pret-yyyy, Baboooo," echoed Bobby Ray.

"Come on, dude." Jerry grabbed the ball from under my shoes and whipped it at Bobby Ray's stomach.

"Wait a sec," said Bobby Ray, nodding toward George. "Maybe the pirate boy was in the circus too!"

Jerry howled.

My hands squeezed into little fists. I was still mad at George for wanting to be a Melon, but . . . my face suddenly felt redder than my red buckle shoes. I stood up. "*What* did you say?"

"He called George a *pirate boy*!" screamed Stephanie.

"Yeah. I called him a pirate. So what?" Bobby Ray tossed the ball back to Jerry and crossed his arms over his chest. He was about twice as tall as the second graders.

I looked over at George, who just looked confused. Neither of us had learned that word yet, but I knew it was horrible. I spit out, "He . . . he is *not* a pirate."

"What is pie rit?" George tilted his head and looked up at the big boys.

"It's someone with a hook for an arm," explained Stephanie. "On a boat!"

George *did* know the word "arm." His smile slowly faded.

Stephanie stomped her foot and tugged at George's hand. "Come on, George. Let's go!"

The sun shined in George's sparkly eyes. "It is . . . okay." His sad mouth suddenly grew into a huge smile. "I am a pie rit!" George swung his good arm all around and laughed. "I am a Pie. A Pie Rit!"

"Whoa, dude," laughed Jerry.

"Don't you see?" I hissed to George in our language. "They're making fun of you. They're being *mean!*" I turned toward Bobby Ray and stepped straight up to him. Our noses would've touched if he hadn't been a head taller than me.

Bobby Ray backed up and smiled. "Wait, wait. Wait a second! You both come from the same country, right?"

George and Stephanie and the second graders inched behind me.

"So, is everybody missing something there? Are people, like, missing their heads and stuff?" Bobby Ray laughed like he might explode. "It's called . . . *Frankenstein Country!*"

Jerry snickered and both of them pulled their T-shirts

up over their heads and walked around with their arms out like monsters.

I looked down at my red buckle shoes. Some of the second graders giggled until Stephanie hushed them up.

George quietly said, "It is from war."

"And the circus," I added.

"What a bunch of bull!" hooted Jerry.

"Total bull!" agreed Bobby Ray. "Let's ask the little pirate."

"Yeah. So was Betti famous in some circus?" Jerry asked. "With her mom and dad?"

George looked up at me. Then he looked at Jerry and Bobby Ray. He squinted his eyes and swung his arm. The rest of us waited until . . . suddenly George said, "Yes. They . . . we are . . . in circus!"

"Oh sure!" said Jerry. "Now the pirate's lying too!"

"He doesn't even know what he's saying!" cackled Bobby Ray. "He doesn't even speak English!" Bobby Ray turned to me again. His eyebrows arched up in scary arrows.

I bugged out my good eye and stared long and hard. The meanest, scariest look my EYE could give.

George said very quietly in our language, "It's okay, Babo. I don't think they understand about our country."

I nodded. George understood everything.

"Why don't you prove it then?" snickered Bobby Ray. "Come on, circus girl!"

"I . . . WILL!" I shouted back.

"What about up there?" Bobby Ray pointed at the monkey bars. "Why don't you do your great circus act with the little pirate right now. That'll work. Close enough to a high wire, right?"

At once, all of us looked over at the monkey bars. They were sort of high-wire lines. In the sky. Long and straight and very skinny. I gulped.

Then I took a deep breath and raised my head in the air. I put my Empty Book back into my orange bag and threw my bag over my shoulder. I bravely stomped through the play yard of Betsy Ross Elementary. I swung my arms back and forth as I walked. Straight to the monkey bars.

I had planned to show them. I had practiced very hard.

But I hadn't planned to prove that I was a star on the monkey bars.

"What? You're gonna do it?" Bobby Ray had to jog to keep up with me.

George was running after me too. And Stephanie. And the second graders.

When I stomped past the little campers, Lucy was hopping around with her sprained foot in the air. She was trying to get the first graders to do circus tricks.

Very bossy. "Betti!" she cried. "Watch us, okay? Watch!" But I think she realized that my circus act was going to be much more exciting. She hobbled after me, and so did the first graders.

Then I saw Mayda and Nanny, the slowest walkers in the whole world, inching their way across the play yard.

Mayda waved. "Hi, Betti!"

"Oh, it *is* Betti, isn't it!" Nanny smiled.

"Where are you going?" asked Mayda.

I pointed.

"The monkey bars?" Mayda squinted behind her crooked pink glasses. "Why?"

"I am . . . in the circus."

Mayda looked at Nanny and touched her hand. Nanny stood still while Mayda followed us: Bobby Ray and me. And half of the day campers.

"Betti, wait!" she called out, but I had to keep going.

From up close the monkey bars looked awfully high, taller than Mr. Buckworth. But I was very talented at climbing trees, almost better than monkeys. I could definitely climb the monkey bars. Easy.

I set my orange bag in the sand and shook off my red buckle shoes. I put my hand on the bottom bar. It was the first of a lot of bars, just like a ladder, that went halfway up to the sky.

Mayda put her hand on one of the bars. "Betti," she

whispered. "You don't have to prove anything. Don't listen to them."

The rest of the Summer Six had come over to see what was happening. Sam and Tabitha and Timmy. I was suddenly very interesting.

Bobby Ray and Jerry were already laughing, flapping their arms and cackling. "Bawk bawk." They didn't understand how brave I was. But I could barely hear them anyway. I climbed up to the next bar, and the next. My feet slipped a little, but I kept climbing.

Ms. Stacy looked up from the volcano table. She probably thought that I was just going to swing on the monkey bars like most Melon kids. She probably thought that Bobby Ray and I were playing together because we were great dudes.

From the top of the monkey bars I could practically see the whole play yard of Betsy Ross Elementary. I was so tall. The tallest girl in the world! All the kids were watching. I could hear the whispers. They were afraid for me; afraid I might fall.

Timmy had his mouth wide open, and even Sam stopped chewing her gum.

George stood at the bottom of the monkey bars with Mayda. He called up quietly in our language, "Babo? Babo, you might fall."

"I won't fall, George. My mama and dad were famous, in the—"

"In the circus. I know. But—"

I started walking on the bar with perfect feet. One step, and then another. I teetered a little. The bar was shiny and slippery. The end of the monkey bar high wire looked very far away. But I took more tiny slow steps; at least three or four.

"Be careful, Babo!" said George.

It didn't feel like I was moving an inch. I wasn't sure I liked being a circus star. Scary. But I could practically hear my audience clapping; I could practically hear the circus music! A light shining on *me*!

I could feel my mama there, waiting for me at the end of my line. I could feel my dad, waiting below to catch me.

Fifteen, sixteen, seventeen steps, almost to the end of the bar. I put my hand up and waved to my whole audience. I was a star and everybody loved me.

Unfortunately, my wave made me lose my balance. It happened in slow motion. My arms were flapping and swinging in circles, and suddenly . . . I was flying! Just like an airplane or a bird or a ghost. Straight toward the ground.

"Hellllp!" I screamed. But on the way down, I accidentally did a flip in the air—not a graceful flip at all, but still a flip—before I landed with a perfect *splat* in the sand.

Everything stood still.

"Babo?" asked George. His knees fell to the ground next to me, and he touched my cheek with his finger.

Mayda kneeled down too. "Are you okay?"

"Whoa, DUDE! That was pretty cool!" said Bobby Ray.

"That was so neat," said Timmy with his wire mouth wide open.

"Totally neat-o," said Jerry.

"She's in the circus, idiot!" Bobby Ray flicked Jerry on the head. "In her country."

"That's my sister," Lucy explained to the first graders.

Ms. Stacy ran fast from the wooden table. "OH!" she cried as she ran. Her eyes looked like they might pop out. "Oh, Betti!"

I had landed right on my orange bag and my Empty Book. The pages of my Empty Book were dirty, my letter from Auntie Moo was crumpled, and everything in my orange bag was squished. I had sand all over my face and my unique circus hair was flying all over the place.

"Betti?" said Mayda and Ms. Stacy at the same time.

"I am a . . . circus . . . girl," I said very quietly, looking up at all of them. "My circus name is . . . Babo."

Birthday Cake

WHEN YOU'RE IN the circus you don't have a birthday.

That's just how it goes. Circus people don't know when they're born and they don't really care. I didn't know how old I was and neither did any of the leftover kids.

But after I'd been in America for almost a whole month, Mrs. Buckworth said that it was America's birthday. "We're going to a party, Betti. Everyone is celebrating the birth of America!"

I imagined an enormous Mama Country giving birth to huge America.

I was glad I'd stayed in America long enough for the birthday party. Day Camp hadn't been so bad after all, now that everyone knew I was a circus star. Sometimes Ms. Stacy's fun activities were even actually fun. Not

as fun as my games, of course. But I decided that staying an extra week or two in America wouldn't hurt anything.

For the birthday party I wore my blue party dress
and my red buckle shoes.

Mrs. Buckworth put her hand on my shoulder and
said, "You look so pretty in your dress, Betti! Beautiful!" My face grew very warm and I smiled, just a little,
because I couldn't help it. Then Mrs. Buckworth asked,
"Would you like to wear your dress too, Lucy?"

"No," replied Lucy, scrunching her face. "No way."

On the way to the birthday party we picked up
Mayda and Nanny, who were waiting for us on Mayda's
tilted porch.

"You have to forgive me," Nanny told the Buckworths. "I walk slower than molasses."

"Don't you worry a bit," said Mrs. Buckworth. She
patted Nanny's hand and linked her arm through
Nanny's.

Once in a while Mayda, who was holding Nanny's
other hand, would say "Oh, Nanny there's a curb right
here," and Nanny would step down. Then Mayda said,
"Oh, Nanny! You should see the purple flowers in this
yard. Practically a hundred of 'em!" Nanny would turn
her milky eyes in that direction and smile. And another
time Mayda said, "Uh-oh. That kid left his skateboard
out again. On your right." And Nanny answered, "I

certainly wouldn't want to take a ride on that, now, would I? I'm young, but not *that* young . . . "

Nanny and Mayda laughed a private laugh as Nanny moved her brown slipper shoes to the left.

We all walked slower than "mole lassies" to Betsy Ross, and when we finally got there, Mr. Buckworth spread out a blanket, next to all sorts of other blankets. George and his mommy showed up and sat down with us. Mayda sat on one side of me and George sat on the other. Nanny talked to Mr. and Mrs. Buckworth, and Lucy played with her freak dolls and waved a flag around.

So many people came to America's birthday party! Some of the Summer Five were there with their parents. Sam waved to me from across the play yard. Her hair had red, white, and blue streaks. Tabitha's parents were round with pink skin, just like her, and Bobby Ray was with his family, and without his backward hat.

The sky was turning dark blue and black. Mrs. Buckworth opened a brown basket and pulled things out one by one. I ate my sandwich and drank my Coke. But the thing I really wanted to eat was Mrs. Buckworth's chocolate cake.

I stared at it for a long time and finally she started cutting it. She put the pieces of cake onto paper plates. I ate my piece in about two seconds. I licked the chocolate goo off my plastic fork and picked the crumbs off my plate. "Ick," I said quietly to the ghosts in the sky. "Ick ick."

"Yummy," said George, with chocolate on his face and all over his teeth.

He only ate half his cake, so I ate his too. Then I ate Mayda's leftover cake, because the ghosts probably thought I was extra good. "Happy birthday, America," I mumbled, spitting chocolate crumbs. This was the best birthday party ever.

Then, all of a sudden, Lucy shouted, "LOOK!"

My head jerked up.

BOOM BOOM BOOM BOOM!

The sky flashed with color. FLASH! Whites and Reds and Blues. Gray smoke filled the air. My body froze and my heart practically stopped. BOOM BOOM BOOM!

I plugged my ears. I squeezed my eyes shut. No, no, no. No one was even ducking on the ground! I covered my whole head with my arms. I remembered every-thing. The circus camp shaking, the helicopters making dust storms, the soldiers hollering and running in big boots through the village and the woods.

"Help . . ." I said in a muffled, tiny voice. Barely a squeak. "Help help."

"Help," said another tiny voice.

George was curled up next to me like a little bug on

the blanket. But no one could hear us. The BOOMS were too loud.

Maybe the Buckworths, and the rest of the Americans, didn't know about BOOMS. All of them were very busy pointing at the sky. "Ooooooo," they cooed. "Ahhhhhh! Ohhhhhhhh!" Some rose to their feet and a few Melons in the audience were actually clapping.

Auntie Moo said there was no war in America, but sometimes war comes out of nowhere. Sometimes it comes for no good reason at all. A people disaster.

George peeked up from the ground. "Babo?" His eyes were scared and sparkly and wet. We looked at each other and nodded. We didn't even have to say a single word.

I grabbed his hand and we shot up from the blanket and . . .

We ran like crazy.

We dodged bicycles and old people waving flags. Instead of trees and prickly vines, we jumped over baskets and blankets and babies. I was much faster than any old soldier. Even George ran sort of fast when he had to. We were like smart night animals that could see everything in the dark. It wasn't our land, we didn't know it like we knew the circus camp, but we were used to running.

Once I tripped and fell hard on the ground, taking George with me. Falling was very dangerous in a war because then you lost time. Then they could catch you.

But George and I stood up in about one second and ran again. My birthday party dress was covered in spaghetti or pizza or something, and my red buckle shoes were covered in cake. Someone shouted, "HEY!" But George and I didn't care.

In one quiet moment I thought I heard: "BETTI! GEORGE?" Maybe it was Mr. Buckworth, it was hard to say. But then the BOOMS started again, louder than the last booms.

George was tired, I could tell, but I kept pulling him along anyway.

"Come on George," I'd say. "Just a little farther."

"Can't we hide here, Babo?"

"No. Just a little farther . . ." I couldn't stop until we found someplace safe.

Then I practically tripped into Mayda and Nanny's wooden bench. It didn't look the same. Melons were sitting on it. But I stopped in my tracks and George had to stop with me.

"Here?" asked George, scrunching his eyes.

"*Under* here."

We squatted down behind it and crawled underneath. We were next to the Melons' feet, but they were too busy ooooohing and ahhhhhing to notice us.

We squeezed each other's hands.

"It's not really a war, is it, Babo?"

"It is! Well, I think it is. I'm pretty sure it is, but—" I wasn't a bit sure.

"My mommy will wonder where we are. And the Buckworths. If they don't know about wars, if they don't know what to do, they'll—"

"I know."

I'd been thinking the same exact thing. I had to go back to save them. That's what happens in a war. Most people try to save each other.

"You have to stay here, George," I whispered.

"But . . . where are you going?"

"Back. To our blanket."

"It's dangerous, Babo," George squeaked. "Auntie Moo always tells us not to move. We're not supposed to make a noise."

"I'm not afraid." I gripped the bottom of the bench with my hands until they turned white. "I'll be right back. With your mommy and the Buckworths. I promise."

"But—"

I closed my good eye. I took a big, big breath. "I'm not afraid." My voice was smaller than a peep. "I'm not afraid. I'm not—"

Before I could even think about being afraid, before I could even stand up, and run like crazy, and save the Buckworths, I saw BIG BLACK BOOTS. By the bench. The boots stopped.

"George! SHHHH!"

I peeked between the Melons' feet and looked up.

I was right.

"George," I whispered, "it's a SOLDIER."

The soldier was wearing a uniform. He was the tallest man I'd ever seen. And he had a gun right on his hip.

"A soldier?"

"Shhhhh."

"Do they have soldiers in America?"

"There are soldiers everywhere, George. Shhhhh."

We stayed completely quiet. It seemed like forever, even though it was just a few minutes. I heard the soldier say, "What a great night. Isn't it, folks?"

And a man sitting on our bench answered, "Sure is, Officer."

George gave me a little nudge with his finger. "Some soldiers are very nice, Babo."

This soldier sounded nice, nice enough, but it was all very confusing. Tricky. And we had to be very, very careful. I inched out from the back of the bench and pulled George up with me. Because I couldn't leave him alone. So we had to run, again.

I thought we were running in the direction of the Buckworths and their blanket. Once I stopped cold and George ran straight into my back. I looked around, I turned in a circle, and took off again in the opposite direction. We ran and ran all over the place. We ran past the volcano table, where people were sitting. We ran past the jungle gym and the monkey bars, where kids were swinging and throwing sand.

Soon George and I stopped running because there were no more people. We were at the end of the play yard. It was quiet and dark in a faraway corner. Very far away from the Buckworths and their cake. All I saw was a small white building, like a pantry or a secret room closet. I opened the door and George and I snuck in.

"Pew," said George. "Pee you."

We plugged our noses.

It was pitch-black inside, but I felt a lock on the door and clicked it shut. We scrunched down. I could barely see the white in George's wide-open eyes.

We waited. We were shivering and it wasn't even cold.

Finally, from the dark I said, "Do you think we'll ever get to go home?"

George touched my cheek with his finger. "To the circus camp?"

Before I could even think about things, I sucked in my breath and answered, "No, to the Buckworths' house. To your mommy's house."

"I hope . . . so." George started crying.

"I am the brave one," I blurted out in a voice smaller than a peep. "But I got—I got so—"

"Scared," said George. He understood everything. "It's okay, Babo. I got scared too. My mommy said it is okay to be scared sometimes."

I rubbed my good eye because it was very watery. I swatted at a few noisy bugs.

George put his arm around me and put his head on my shoulder. "It's okay, Babo. It's okay."

He took a deep breath. *"There is byooteeful girl. Her name Babo. She has friend name George. They swim. In George swim poo. At George house. Babo is . . . circus girl. In America. She byooteeful . . . star . . ."*

Lost in America

WE FELL ASLEEP, just like that.

When I woke up the explosions had stopped. There was perfect quiet except for voices calling from far away. Maybe soldiers' voices, it was hard to say. But I could tell that most of the people were gone. By now all the Americans were probably hiding or running. Everything was probably on fire. Or, if there wasn't a war, they had all just gone home.

I had been bad at the Buckworths' so they'd send me back. Very very bad. I had planned to run away. I had been on guard at all times, just like I was supposed to. I had waited for the right time to escape. Now George and I were alone and I felt sad because I couldn't help it.

We were leftover kids. Again.

I thought of Rooney drooling all over me, and Puddles peeing in my room. I thought of Nanny with her special eyes, and Mayda with her special dreams. I wouldn't get to hear Lucy talking in all sorts of crazy voices, or Mr. and Mrs. Buckworth telling me that everything was going to be okay. "You may not love us yet, little tiger, but we still love you."

They didn't put me in the zoo for telling stories about the war. They didn't lock me in the TV or throw me away. They didn't want me to forget everything.

I squeezed my eyes tight, really, really tight. I hoped all of them wouldn't miss me too much, and I tried not to think about missing them forever.

Then someone knocked on the door. Our little building shook.

George sat up fast. I squeezed his hand. Not a peep.

Knock. KNOCK, KNOCK.

"Kids?" said the husky deep voice. "Are you in there?"

I knew it right away. The soldier's voice.

My good eye grew huge even though I couldn't see a single thing in the dark. I squeezed George's hand even tighter, which made him squirm.

"BETTI?" There was another loud knock. The soldier tried opening the door. "George?" The handle jerked up and down.

"He knows our names, Babo," George whispered in my ear. "He knows us."

"Shhhhh. That could be even worse."

Finally the knocking stopped. The handle stopped shaking and I heard big boots marching away in the dirt.

I let out a sigh and George whimpered a little.

"Maybe he wants to help us, Babo."

"I don't know. I don't know." I used to think that Melons tricked people, but not a single American had tricked me. Very confusing.

We were quiet.

Suddenly I heard the handle shaking again. I heard the lock click. The door opened a crack and then it swung all the way open. I gasped. I could see stars in the sky. I could see the jungle gym and the monkey bars far across the play yard.

The soldier never would've found us. Or he wouldn't have found us if it hadn't been for George.

"I am HERE!" cried George in English. He was standing outside our little building. "It is ME!" he hollered louder. "My name is . . . GEORGE!"

POLICE MAN.

He is here to help people.

That's what he told us as he held our small hands in his enormous hands.

"Your parents have been worried sick about you kids. We've all been looking everywhere," he said. "Inside the school, all over the neighborhood, in all the parking lots. We figured those fireworks must've scared you . . ."

It was Mayda who saw us first. "Betti!"

"Is it her?" cried Nanny. "Are they okay?"

And in about one second Mrs. Buckworth was there, and Mr. Buckworth sprinted over with Lucy, and George's mommy ran from the front doors of Betsy Ross Elementary. George dashed straight toward her with his arm out and almost knocked her over. He started sobbing and his mommy sobbed too.

"Betti, oh sweetie, we were *so* worried!" cried Mrs. Buckworth.

"Shhhhh. You're safe now," said Mr. Buckworth, hugging me like a big bear.

"I was *so* afraid you were lost forever!" wailed Lucy.

And me? All I could choke out was, "I was *so*—worried too. But you are—saved."

If anyone saw me in the center of this family circle, everyone hugging and crying and laughing, they may have thought it looked exactly like an American love story.

The Best Circus in the World

Dear Auntie Moo . . .

I am worried. I worry about the war and the soldiers and the bombs and the leftover children. And I really worry about you, even though you told me not to. I think about you every day.

Sometimes life in America is crazy. And a little dangerous. But not dangerous like our country.

The Buckworths promised me that someday we will travel back there. The whole family, even Lucy. We will go on a vacation but not to the pretty places. We will come to see you, as soon as the war cools off.

The Buckworths are very nice and they love me. They found me when I was lost and they don't care that I am broken. You were right. I am okay.

I will miss you forever and always. Until I see you again.

      Love Betti

P.S. I will never forget my old name.

TODAY IS MY birthday.

Mr. and Mrs. Buckworth asked me if I would like to pick my own very special day. Any day of the whole year. So I picked the last day of summer, after Day Camp and before the start of fifth grade at Betsy Ross Elementary.

Last night I was sitting on the floor petting Rooney and Puddles, the Buckworths were sitting on the sofa, and Lucy was flipping fast through channels on the TV. That's when I saw something on TV and I said, "Wait."

People were running. Things were on fire. Smoke rose from the ground. Dirty children had holey clothes, buildings were burned out, and rubble was every-where. There were faces crying. I could see every tear up close. I could almost touch them. It wasn't a Big Mouth TV story. It was real. I knew immediately it was my country.

I climbed right between Mr. and Mrs. Buckworth on the fluffy sofa.

I was trying to be very brave but then . . . my good eye started to water. I was thinking about Auntie Moo and the leftover kids. I was thinking about Sister Baroo, who was tough as tree bark. I was thinking about Old Lady Suri at the bean stand, and Big Uncle in his beat-up taxi, and all the people George and I saw in the bombed villages. And I was thinking about the circus people. If there were any left in my country.

"Do you think my country will always be broken?" I asked in a tiny sniffling voice.

The Buckworths thought about this. Finally Mrs. Buckworth said, "Someday it will be okay, Betti." She breathed a deep breath. "I'm not sure when, but someday your country will have peace again."

Mr. Buckworth pulled me onto his lap even though I was about eleven years old and way too big. Mrs. Buckworth took my head in her arms and ran her fingers through my crazy hair. Lucy crawled away from the TV with her freak dolls. She looked up at me and tilted her head. Then she bounced her dolls up my leg and on my toes, even where my toes were missing. "It will be okay, Betti. Don't cry."

So then I cried some more. I cried and cried and I couldn't even stop.

But Auntie Moo believes that the world is beautiful, and I am her eyes. So today, on my special day, I cannot only think about the bad things and the sad things. I have to believe the world is beautiful too.

Mr. Buckworth took me to the post office and we

mailed off lots of big presents to the circus camp. He told me that I could mail things to Auntie Moo and the leftover kids anytime, even though it might take a very long time to get there.

So . . . I put a brand-new book of English words into the big box for Auntie Moo, along with my letter. I put some furry stuffed circus bears and cookies and marshmallows into the boxes for the leftover kids, and lots of stuff into the boxes for Sister Baroo's Mission: dried food and flip-flops and some medicine for when anyone got sick. I also put pictures in the boxes, some that I had drawn myself, and some that Mayda had taken of me in America with her camera.

Just before Mr. Buckworth and I sealed up my presents, I took my Empty Book out of Auntie Moo's box. I decided to keep it. It wasn't empty anymore; it was filled with all sorts of things, all of my stories about living in America. Maybe I'd want to look at it someday so I could remember.

Then my special birthday party started like this:

I got to swim in George's purple plastic pool. George's mommy brought it over to the Buckworths' backyard. Lucy swam, and so did Mayda and Stephanie. George and I swam too, even though George's purple pool was very small and we were all squished. We splashed around and threw water on each other and got all wet. Rooney and Puddles got all wet too.

George got to pick a birthday too and his birthday was yesterday. George told his mommy that he wanted a monkey more than anything in the whole world. George's mommy said that pet monkeys were a little hard to find in America. So today George got to pick a puppy and he didn't want just any old puppy. He wanted Puddles, even though Puddles is an old lady and definitely not a puppy. But old ladies are very special in our country; they are the wise ones. When George held Puddles in his arms, George barked and Puddles wisely woofed back and everyone laughed.

The best part of my birthday, though, was my very famous circus in the Buckworths' backyard. I made the sign myself. It would have been very useful for scaring off hungry scavengers from the bean field.

The Best Circus in the World.

And the rest of my party guests arrived for our show.

Mayda was the first beautiful circus star.

She belongs in the circus. She comes to play with me all the time now. Especially on the days when Nanny is sick. Mrs. Buckworth likes for us to play at my house, instead of Mayda's, so we don't get into big trouble.

Every time Mayda comes over she tells me stories about her dad and all the places they've lived, and she tells me how she imagines her mom, the lost photographer with a new family. And I tell Mayda Big Mouth stories about . . . me.

I told her how Auntie Moo found me eating lizards when the circus camp was burning like a bonfire. I told her how the leftover kids arrived, one by one, and how I had the very important job of being the brave leader. I told her about us walking down to the market every week, even though we didn't have money to buy anything, and about George and me riding away in the Chevy taxi. I told her most of Old Lady Suri's stories, too, even though so many of them weren't exactly true. The best one was about my mama and dad, my circus people.

"That one's a nice story, Betti," Mayda said one day. "And who knows?" She shrugged. "Maybe it's true."

Mayda understands a lot.

At my birthday party she was supposed to be the Animal Trainer, so she tried to get Rooney to jump over a swing on the swing set. But Rooney smiled at her and drooled. Then Mayda tried to get Puddles to jump through a plastic hoop, but Puddles just licked Mayda's shoes. Mayda sighed as she took her bow, and Rooney lifted his leg and peed on Mrs. Buckworth's flowers.

Lucy was next. Mrs. Buckworth let her wear eye makeup because it was a special day. Lucy decided her act would be a Famous Puppet Show. She made all of her freak dolls, with teeny-tiny puppet heads, bounce up and down with different voices. Jessie Lynn still wasn't married because Ramon liked Roller Derby Tina better. Lucy's puppet show really didn't make any sense, but she had quite a talent with her Big Mouth.

I, of course, got to be the special final act. I got to walk on my high wire line in the sky. Actually, the line Mr. Buckworth made was wider than both of my feet, and lower than Lucy's knees. It was a board. Hardly anyone could fall off Mr. Buckworth's fat board, not even me.

I walked very carefully anyway.

I had almost made it all the way across, which is just how we practiced it. That's when George, my circus partner, was supposed to run out, do a turn, and catch me as I took a dramatic leap off the end. Unfortunately, George got carried away.

He twirled and twirled like crazy, and flapped his arms around, and made loud bird noises. "Caw caw QUACK QUACK!" He had so much fun that he knocked into me and made me lose my balance. He tried to catch me, but he wasn't used to his brand-new arm—which he'd had fixed in the hospital—that looked almost real.

This morning Mrs. Buckworth told me that a doctor of eyes could possibly fix my broken eye too. But I told her that I'd have to think about it. "Maybe when I'm old," I said. "Like in the nine grade." I like my fish eye, grayer than smoke or a rainy day. It lets me see halfway into the past and at least a little into the future: my old life at the circus camp and my new life with the Buckworths. My eye gives me good luck.

But this time? Well, not so lucky.

George and I fell together into a heap on the ground. The funny makeup on our faces was all messed up, and my funny orange wig flew off. George, with his legs sprawled over me like a wishbone, laughed as if this was the best day of his life.

Then, suddenly . . . I heard it. Clapping. It shook the soft green grass and the swing set. It was louder than a noisy monsoon.

I saw Ms. Stacy and the Summer Five clapping in my audience. Timmy didn't have freaky teeth anymore because his metal wires were all gone. They were straight and white as river stones. Sam was there with some purple streaks in her hair and Tabitha brought me a fake stuffed cat for my birthday present. Bobby Ray and Jerry clapped too, because they liked me. Or, they at least liked me a little because now they called me Dude.

Lenore the adoption expert lady was there, clapping and smiling. She probably felt that I had adapted, at least a little, to being adopted.

George's mommy was there clapping and so was Mayda's dad. Mayda's dad took the day off from work, both jobs, so he could see Mayda in the circus and meet me: Mayda's new friend. And Nanny, in her dark gray glasses, was clapping. "Marvelous," she kept saying. "Just marvelous." She could see all sorts of things.

My mom and dad were clapping too. My dad, of course, was doing a funny disco dance to the circus music.

"Mom!" I called out, sniffling. "Did you see that?"

So my mom came over and checked me for scratches or scrapes. None. I was a very clumsy circus girl. My mom just smiled at me and looked happy because she knew I was happy.

Today—my birthday—I've decided to start calling Mr. and Mrs. Buckworth my mom and dad.

And who knows? Maybe I'll like it. Maybe I already do.

Auntie Moo says that there's a reason you find a person, and a reason that a person finds you. That's why we were so lucky that she found me and I found her when I was toddling around. And George and the leftover kids found both of us. Well, that's exactly how I feel now. I feel lucky that I found Mayda after I kicked Bobby Ray at Day Camp. I feel extra lucky that my mom and dad, the Buckworths, found me at my circus camp.

"Babo?" whispered George. "I think we're going to be friends forever." He giggled and touched my red clown nose with his new finger. "Don't you, Babo?"

"Probably," I said with a big sigh. "Yes."

I looked up at the sky and there wasn't a single thing falling. It was a blue sky. I squinted and blinked as the sun sparkled in my good eye and my lucky broken eye. And finally . . . I started to laugh like crazy.

(BLAH BLAH BLAH)
THE END

A Note from the Author

DEAR READER,

You may be wondering where in fact Betti comes from? You may want to pummel me over the head, feed me to Cindi the lion, and smoosh me in the center of a fire circle for not telling you through this whole entire book.

Well, it's not that I've intentionally played tricks on you or kept secrets. The problem is that I haven't been able to name her country. And trust me, I've tried and tried and tried.

But there are far too many people disasters—wars—happening in our world right now. There are too many countries, like Betti's country, where kids have to watch the sky for things falling, and listen for the booms. Their homes have skeleton walls and shot-out windows. And people they know have disappeared or been killed, like Betti's circus family. That's what happens sometimes during a war. But, remember, what also happens is that people try to save each other.

I've worked in some of these war-torn places, and I've worked with kids like George and Betti. Little tigers, filled with fear and love and broken eyes, who are still trying to believe that this is a beautiful world. To name Betti's country would mean that I'd be circling one small spot on a very large map—and that doesn't seem fair—when there are so many strong and courageous kids all over the world.

Maybe, dear reader, you will have a much easier time naming Betti's exact place, and the color of her face. Maybe you'd like to name the texture of her trees, and the food she eats, and the language she speaks.

You are welcome to, if you wish. Wherever she comes from, please be kind.

Sincerely,

Lisa Railsback

Acknowledgments

To Rebecca Sherman, my lovely agent, who has courageously supported me and fought for my work like a little tiger, and to Kate Harrison, my lovely editor, who has tremendous insight and had sweet Betti dreams from the beginning.

To the Michener Center for Writers at the University of Texas at Austin for giving me three free years to make a transition from the stage to this page, and to my professors there, Suzan Zeder and Shirley Lukenbill, who patiently read the early bad Betti drafts.

To the Anderson Center for Interdisciplinary Studies, which gave me a perfectly peaceful month surrounded by art, and beauty, and artists, while I finished revising Betti.

To my mama, Patricia, who doesn't have a tail, but

who has held out her arms when I've reached the end of my line, and to my dad, Thomas, who has been there to catch me.

To my sisters, who have humorously contributed to my circus life; to my nieces and nephews, who are tough literary critics; and to my friends, who have shared their Big Mouth stories about being writers for years and years.

Finally, to my old dog, Rooney, who lovingly drooled on my feet under my desk, and to my nana, Irene, who wisely saw color in dark places.

I thank you.